The Land of Dragons

TALES OF DELTORA

Emily Rodda

with illustrations by

Marc McBride

SCHOLASTIC INC.

New York Toronto London Auckland Sydney

Mexico City New Delhi Hong Kong Buenos Aires

ISBN 0-439-87785-7

Text copyright © Emily Rodda, 2005.
Deltora Quest concept and characters copyright © Emily Rodda.
Deltora Quest is a registered trademark of Rin Pty Ltd.
Illustrations copyright © Scholastic Australia Pty Ltd, 2005.
Cover and interior illustrations by Marc McBride.

All rights reserved. Published by Scholastic Inc., 557 Broadway, New York, NY 10012, by arrangement with Scholastic Press, an imprint of Scholastic Australia.

SCHOLASTIC and associated logos are trademarks and/or registered trademarks of Scholastic Inc.

12 11 10 9 8 7 6 5 4 3 2   6 7 8 9 10 11/0

Printed in Singapore.
First American edition, May 2006

Contents

The Girl with the Golden Hair

A Note from Josef

his book of tales contains the secret history of Deltora. That is a startling claim, I know, but it is true.

The first volume of *The Deltora Annals* contains all the folktales of the seven tribes. Among them are the ancient Jalis legends known as the Tenna Birdsong Tales.

Scholars of the past dismissed the Birdsong Tales as nothing more than charming fairy tales. Possibly they were correct in the case of fables like "The Girl with the Golden Hair"— the bittersweet story of a girl who gives her golden hair to a dragon to save her lover. In other cases, however, they were certainly unwise, for lately we have learned that many of the Tenna Birdsong Tales contain much more than a grain of truth. And, looking at them further, and at last understanding the clues within them, I have made an amazing discovery.

The Tenna Birdsong Tales are not just stories of make-believe people and places. If they are read carefully, in the correct order, they actually tell the story of our own land in ancient times.

I have selected those that most clearly show the story's thread. They make up the first part of this book, and are copied exactly from the *Annals*. By long tradition, the Birdsong Tales are always told in the same words, and I would never be so bold as to change them.

The clever reader will soon see the clues I have seen and understand what I mean when I say the tales reveal Deltora's secret history. The reader, indeed, may wonder why this discovery was not made long ago.

I can only say that great truths often seem obvious once they are pointed out. But like a needle in a pile of hay, they are sometimes strangely difficult to see beforehand.

The remaining stories in this book tell of the rise of the great Adin, and the creation of the magic Belt of Deltora. These tales are in my own words, and are based on the writings of Adin and others. In many ways, they also reveal a secret history, because most of the information they contain has never before been seen outside the pages of *The Deltora Annals* itself.

When first I began this book, King Lief promised that it would be published widely. It pleases me to think that my work may help bring Deltoran history to life, not only for the people of this land, but perhaps for people of other lands, also, in time to come.

Our story is rich and strange. In my mind I see it as a vast picture woven of many strands. There is the broad, mysterious strand of the land itself, with all its beauties and its terrors. There is the dark strand of the Shadow Lord's hunger to dominate and destroy. There is the bright strand of courage, hope, and heroes. There is the glittering strand of magic and prophecy and dreams. And woven through them all, like circling bands of rainbow light, are the strands that mark the paths of dragons.

Read on, and see them for yourselves.

In faith —

Josef

Palace Librarian in the Time of King Lief

The Land of Dragons

A Tenna Birdsong Tale

Once, when the world was young, the sea was alive with monsters and all the lands were islands. The islands were many, but most were far apart. To birds flying high, they looked like jeweled eggs, cupped in nests of foam and scattered on a broad blue plain.

Some of the islands were small, and some were large, but all were the prisoners of the sea. For the sea was vast and deadly — an endless waste of cruel water, seething with teeth, spines, cold black eyes, and tentacles that coiled like hungry tongues.

One of the largest and strangest of the islands was called by its people the Land of Dragons, for dragons ruled its skies. The people were divided into seven tribes, and each tribe kept to its own territory. Even between neighboring tribes there was little trade, marriage, or friendship. Instead, there was suspicion and, all too often, war, for food and fresh water were not divided equally among the territories, and life was hard for many.

But if the people of the Land of Dragons knew little about their neighbors, they knew nothing at all of the world beyond their shores. For all they knew, indeed, they were alone beneath the vast dome of the sky.

To their north was another island, richly green and

ringed with pure white sand. At dawn, at noon, and at sunset, a faint fluting sound drifted from this island like a beckoning call. But no dragons soared in its skies, and no living thing was ever seen moving on its white shore.

Imprisoned by the perilous sea that surrounded them, the people of the Land of Dragons could only gaze at the misty green island from afar. They wondered about it, and many tales and legends grew around it.

Old folk said that it was their own island's twin, but a twin that was perfectly good, lacking the evils and dangers of the Land of Dragons. It was said that the Twin was a magic place. It was said that hidden deep within the green were crystal palaces, lush gardens, and pools of sweet water that mirrored the sky. It was said that within this paradise lived wondrous beings who were wise and good.

There were those who laughed and did not believe the tales. There were others who longed to see the wonders of the Twin for themselves, without hoping that they ever would. But now and then a brave soul — or a fool — would make a boat and set out to discover the truth.

Not one of these adventurers was ever seen again. The Twin was farther away than it seemed. No matter how early a craft set out, darkness always overtook it while it was still in the open sea, so it was lost to sight. When watchers in the Land of Dragons looked again at dawn, the sea was always empty.

Some people clung to the hope that the lost ones had reached the magic isle in the night and now were safe in bliss among the crystal palaces and the flowers. But most suspected that the sea had claimed them, and in their dreams they saw bones lying gnawed and white in deep, cloudy water amid the splinters of wood, a rusting anchor, and the rotting rags of sails.

For the beasts of the sea were fearful. They writhed and fought without ceasing. They were savage, and

For the beasts of the sea were fearful . . .

always hungry. Only the dragons did not fear them. Only the dragons dared to fish far from shore, changing the churning water to steam with their fiery breath.

Some of the sea monsters hunted the fish that swarmed beneath the surface of the waves, birds that swooped too near, and humans who strayed too far from land. Many of these beasts were known by the people of the Land of Dragons — Sea Serpent, Sea Wolf, Mirodan, Strangler, Vulture Fish, Bird Bane, and Deadeye were just a few of the names that struck dread in every heart.

Some monsters invaded the land to seek prey, swimming up rivers, lurking in caves, or crawling onto rocks and sandy shores. These beasts, too, were named by the people who feared them. Some of the names were Kobb, Kreel, Stinger, Bubbler, Blood Creeper, and Death Spinner or Glus.

But the largest and most ghastly of all the monsters of the sea skulked in the depths, carving grottoes and palaces for themselves from the rock of the seabed and feasting in the darkness. No human ever saw them and lived, so they remained nameless.

And so it was, when the world was young. The monsters of the sea ruled, and thought their reign would never end. The dragons were the glittering masters of the sky. The people lived in fear, and clung to the land. And the land waited, biding its time.

Fire and Water

A Tenna Birdsong Tale

or countless ages the sea seemed unchanging to the people of the Land of Dragons. That was because they saw only its surface, gleaming in the sun by day and heaving black beneath the stars at night.

They could not see that, far below, the nameless monsters — blind, jealous, and bloated — were burrowing deeper and deeper into the seabed. They did not know that in places not far from their island the rock of the seabed had grown thin as an eggshell, and that the fiery core of the earth below, hotter than a dragon's breath, was preparing to belch forth its fury.

The tribe of the west, a grave, black-haired people wise in the ways of magic, sensed that a great terror was coming. In their meetinghouse of woven branches, the leaders scattered fortune-telling stones. They saw that the stones meaning fire, water, death, and marriage fell together time after time. But they did not know what to think of it.

The dragons, too, sensed that change was coming. They felt the land quiver with the knowledge. They smelled it in the air. But they did not wonder what it meant. They merely watched — and waited.

And there came a morning — a beautiful, still morning when the sky was like a perfect blue bowl set over a sea as smooth as glass — when the birds and insects of the island fell silent, and the beasts in the fields raised their heads.

The dragons knew it was time. In a great, glittering rush, they took to the air. They rose from every corner of the island: from the rocks and dunes of the west and east; from the sandy shores of the south; from the forests, plains, and hills of the center; and from the cliffs of the north. There were thousands of them — thousands upon thousands. There were so many that their great, leathery wings, glimmering with all the colors of the rainbow, blocked out the sun.

The people of the seven tribes gaped in terror. The earth trembled beneath their feet. The sky was dark with dragons. There was a low sound from the north, as if the sea itself was growling. And then those who that day were near the northern shores saw the sea turn white. The beasts of the sea were whipping the water to foam as they struggled to flee.

But it was too late to flee. With a mighty roar, the sea-bed split, and fire belched upward.

The sea boiled. Great slabs of melting rock burst through the churning surface in a hurricane of steam, hurled into the air as if by a giant hand.

The Land of Dragons quaked. Great cracks opened in the earth. Hills fell to rubble and new hills grew. The air was thick with steam, and pale, slimy dead things fell from the sky like rain. And still fire and water met and raged beneath the sea, each battling to quench the other.

The people howled like beasts and fell to the ground, clapping their hands over their ears. The sound was frightful. The sights were sights of terror. They heard a thunderous, crashing groan of rock, and the island shuddered. They thought the end of their world had come.

In a great, glittering rush, they took to the air.

But their world had not ended. It had merely changed. And when those who were left alive crawled to their feet in the exhausted silence that fell upon the land at last, they saw how it was — at least in part.

The sands and bays of the northern coast were gone — buried beneath towering mountains of rock torn from the seabed. The high, rugged headland of the northwest had become one peak among many that now stretched in a grim, unbroken line from west to east.

And on that first day, what was behind those mountains, only the dragons knew. Only the dragons, flying high above, had seen the space between the Land of Dragons and the green island to its north disappear as the cracked seabed collapsed and folded in on itself, while the water turned to steam. Only they saw the two islands collide, their coasts forever sealed together by melted rock and the weight of the new mountain range.

The twin islands had become one. Fire, water, and death had brought about a marriage, just as the stones of the west had foretold.

But the seven tribes of the Land of Dragons knew none of this on that first day, and if they had known, they would not have cared. Mourning their dead, mourning the destruction of their homes and villages, they wandered their changed territories like lost souls.

Nothing was as it had been. For seven days and seven nights the sun was masked by clouds, and salt water fell like fine rain. The thick air stank of death. And the dragons did not come to land.

But on the eighth day, the rain stopped. A light breeze came and blew away the clouds and the stink of death. The sun shone again, and people raising their faces gratefully to its light and warmth saw the dazzle of rainbow colors as the dragons swooped to earth.

And on that day, one by one, each tribe made a

discovery. The great cracks that had opened in the earth had created hills and valleys, caves and rivers where none had existed before. But they had done more than that. In every territory, the splitting rock had given up a great secret — a wondrous gem from deep within the earth.

The people of each tribe marveled as they felt the power of the gift the land had given them — a talisman born of its own suffering, promising protection and a new beginning.

And that day did indeed mark a new beginning for the Land of Dragons. New rivers ran now, from the mountains to the sea. The earth grew rich and fertile. The land blossomed, beasts fattened, and fruit hung heavy on the vines. The people of the coast went out in boats and caught fish, for vast numbers of the sea monsters had died in the battle of fire and water, and their reign of terror had ended.

The green land on the other side of the mountains remained a mystery. The islands had become one, but the two peoples were as far apart as ever. The mountains that separated them were as fearsome a barrier as the sea had once been. Monsters torn from the deep survived in dripping lairs deep within the rocks. In the cold, wet darkness they grew strong, bred, and changed. So the mountains became places of terror, the refuge of scoundrels, bandits, and murderers who needed to hide where no one dared to follow.

Some of the curious from the Land of Dragons went around the mountain barrier by sea. They drew their boats up on the shores of the beautiful green land they knew as the Twin. They smelled its sweet air and stepped onto its white sand. But try as they might, they could move no farther. Powerful magic held them back, and at last they were forced to leave with their curiosity unsatisfied and their gifts of friendship ungiven.

The beings of the Twin had no wish to trade, tell tales, or know their neighbors, it seemed. They did not desire company.

So after a time the people of the Land of Dragons almost forgot that another land existed behind the mountains of the north. They looked outward for their pleasure. They sailed the ocean far and wide. They found other lands and brought back treasures, ideas, strange foods, and beasts and birds from far away. But at home they rarely strayed beyond their borders. At home, each tribe stayed in its own place.

And each tribe jealously guarded its talisman, the gem of power that had been the land's gift after the time of trial. Each tribe thought itself especially rich and favored, for it did not know the other talismans existed.

The dragons knew, but each dragon drew strength only from the gem of its own territory and cared nothing for the rest. And the land knew, but it could not speak to those who would not hear. So again it waited, biding its time.

The Four Sisters

A Tenna Birdsong Tale

Long ago, on a beautiful island set in a silver sea, there lived four sisters whose voices were as sweet as their hearts were pure. Their names were Flora, Viva, Aqua, and Terra, and they had lived on the island so long that they had forgotten the number of the years.

The sisters loved to sing together, and their voices flowed over the island like soft, warm breezes by night and by day. Now and then a ship passed by, but to most of the sailors the sisters' song was like whispering leaves, lapping water, drifting sand, and the soft, secret rustling of small animals in the grass. The few who claimed to hear sweet voices were mocked by their fellows. But they knew what they had heard, and they never forgot it until their dying day.

It so happened that a sorcerer came to that island, searching for a place to call his own. He heard the singing and hated it, as he hated all things good and beautiful, for although he was still young in his years, he was old in his wickedness.

He seized the four sisters and imprisoned each on a separate corner of the island. But the sisters still sang to one another from afar, and their song continued to bathe the island in peace and beauty by night and by day.

Maddened with rage, the sorcerer drew his cloak of shadows around him and took up his magic staff. He stormed to each of the island's corners in turn and struck the sisters down, one by one.

First Flora's voice ceased. Then Viva's. Then Aqua's. For a time Terra sang on alone. But when her voice, too, was stopped, the island went silent.

And only then did the sorcerer realize what he had done. For in the very center of the island, hidden deep within the earth, was a vile and hideous beast. Soothed by the singing of the four sisters, the beast had slept for centuries.

Now it awoke, in all its fury.

It rose, roaring, from its bed beneath the earth. It tore down the trees, crushed the small beasts, fouled the spring, and smashed the mountains. It cracked the very rock on which the island rested, and the island began to sink.

In terror the sorcerer leaped into the silver sea. He conjured up a boat with a gray sail marked with red, and sailed away into the east to find new lands to conquer.

The waves closed over the island, and it has never been seen by human eye from that day to this. A few of the sailors who pass that way still claim to hear sweet voices singing beneath the water. They are mocked by their fellows, who hear only the sound of wind and waves. But the few know what they heard, and they never forget it, until their dying day.

Now it awoke, in all its fury.

The Tale of the Sorcerer

A Tenna Birdsong Tale

One dark night, a great storm raged on the wild west coast of the Land of Dragons, but the people of that territory went to their beds without fear. They were far away from the furious sea, safe and warm in their strong white city built by magic. They slept peacefully, knowing that the great amethyst that was their talisman protected them from harm.

So only the fish and the birds of the shore heard the crash as a boat with a broken mast and a tattered gray sail marked in red was blown onto the treacherous finger of rock that stretched deep into the silver sea.

The people slept on as the boat splintered in the waves. They slept on as its sail was torn to rags by the wind. They slept on as the rain ceased and the moon sailed out from behind the clouds.

But when a drenched, cloaked figure crawled out of the sea and sprawled half dead upon the shore, a shiver ran through the white city, and the people woke. The storm had passed, but a shadow had fallen on their land, and they knew it was far more dangerous than any storm.

As one they rose from their beds and moved to the center of the city where the great amethyst lay on its table of stone. They stood together — every man, woman, and child. And their minds met.

Far away, on the shore, the sodden figure groaned and flinched. Rage mingled with fear and shock as he felt the banishing spell take hold of him, felt his limbs begin to tremble, and felt his heart go cold. Someone wanted him gone. Someone was daring to defy his will.

He was a mighty sorcerer, but he had been sadly weakened. The banishing spell was strong. He knew that he could not resist it for long. He refused to be driven back to the sea, which had stolen his magic staff and almost taken his life. He closed his eyes, summoned all that remained of his strength, and took himself from the place of torment, took himself north, instinctively knowing which way to go.

When he opened his eyes he was in a rocky place, and mountains towered above him. The agony of the banishing spell had not merely weakened, but had gone — gone as if it had never been — for the people of the marble city were satisfied. The shadow had lifted from their territory. Where it went after that was no concern of theirs.

The sorcerer straightened his shoulders and smiled. He turned to survey the land that he would make his own.

And crouched before him was a dragon, vast and terrible. Its green scales glittered in the moonlight. Its eyes were like great, flat emeralds, and steam drifted from its dripping jaws. The sorcerer felt its power and knew that he could not destroy it.

So he tried to bargain with it. He offered it all the treasure his dark magic could provide if only it would serve him.

The green dragon's eyes narrowed. "Dragons are servants to no man, sorcerer," it hissed. "We are the servants of the land. And the land has no use for you. Begone!"

It breathed fire, and the rocks sizzled. The sorcerer felt the heat sear his flesh, and his robes began to smoke. He removed himself from the dragon's sight, retreating deep into the mountains.

The dragon did not follow him. And so the sorcerer learned that the depths of the mountains were not dragon territory. There he was safe.

In a dank cave he rested, and grew stronger. The foul things that skulked amid the rocks were no threat to him. They fawned upon him, drawn to his dark power.

The sorcerer was safe, but he was not content. Rage burned within him. He left the cave and prowled the mountains from one end to the other, awaiting his chance to swoop down upon the land. On the way he met more foul creatures, and also men and women — the ragged groups of bandits and killers who haunted the mountain depths.

Rejoicing in his wickedness, these desperate souls gathered around him and followed him, willing him to triumph. The sorcerer despised them, but he took them and used them for his purposes. They told him everything they knew of the land they hated and the people they preyed upon. They showed him all the secret ways that led down through the mountains into the Land of Dragons.

But their secrets were no secrets to the protectors of the land. Every way the sorcerer tried was guarded by dragons, and no dragon would let him pass.

In fury he turned away from the Land of Dragons, telling himself that it must wait. He ordered his followers to lead him through the mountains to the other side. The land there would be his first domain. His followers whimpered, but he snarled and burned their minds until they did his will. So they led him to a place where he could see the beautiful green land that lay to the mountains' north.

It breathed fire, and the rocks sizzled.

Then the sorcerer found that this land, too, was barred to him. No dragons guarded its borders, but the very air was magic; morning, noon, and night there came a sound that repelled him and pierced him to the bone.

Now his fury and hatred were so great that his heart was like a burning coal in his chest.

He swore to own the lands that had defied him. He swore to own them, every stick and stone. He swore to tear out their hearts. He swore to slaughter their beasts, smash their rocks, and burn their trees. He swore to crush their people under his heel. He would force them to call him master.

Raging, he returned to his den in the west, and his followers stumbled after him, for by now they were slaves to his will and were his creatures body and soul.

For years they served him as he plunged deeper into dark magic, as he gathered knowledge of his prey and made his plans. He made them crawl before him. He treated them like beasts, but none of them dared leave him. They kept company with the vile monsters of the rocks, living only to do their master's bidding. And they watched in terror as his power grew.

The Dragon's Egg

A Tenna Birdsong Tale

One day, the sorcerer of the mountains left his den and flew to a high, snowy peak from which he could see the lands below. He gazed down at the green land to the north of the mountains and smiled. For years he had watched it. He had learned the source of its strength and found out its weaknesses. He had made plans for it, and soon those plans would be put into action.

He was strong now, very strong. His hands held the power of life and death. He could wither growing things with a touch. He could create half life from scraps of bone and flesh. In the green land, his schemes would have room to grow. And then . . .

The sorcerer turned and looked down at the Land of Dragons with a sneer. No doubt, the dragons believed they had defeated him. They could think what they liked. His revenge could wait, and would be all the sweeter for it. In time, the dragons would be destroyed and their land would be his. If only he could find a way . . .

Ice was forming on the sorcerer's face and on his hands. Cold and heat no longer troubled him, but he was still mortal. He knew it was time to return to his den before his body froze. He prepared to leave, but just as he was about to do so, his foot touched something round beneath the snow. Curious, he scraped the snow away. And there he saw an egg, lying in a nest of stones.

The egg was huge, with a thick, lumpy, speckled shell. The sorcerer's heart leaped. A dragon's egg!

He bent and lifted the egg in his hands. It was cold — cold as ice. But he knew it was alive. He could almost see the small heart beating beneath the mottled shell. He could almost see the curved, transparent claws, the spiny tail coiled around the sleeping, infant body.

How often had he sent his sniveling followers out to search for dragons' eggs? How many times had they returned, empty-handed, to face his wrath? And now, the thing he had been searching for, the key to his destruction of the Land of Dragons, was in his hands.

"The dragon in this egg will know me as its master," the sorcerer said to the cold gray sky. "From its scales, teeth, and flesh I will create a new race of dragons — a dragon army that will fight for me, destroying their kin in my service. And the Land of Dragons will be mine."

He put the egg beneath his cloak and took himself back to his den. So gleeful was he, his mind so filled with plans, that he did not remember that dragons' nests were always lined with human hair.

In the warmth of his den, he took the egg from beneath his cloak and placed it in a bowl on the table. He ordered his servants to build up the fire. Then he sat in a chair — and waited.

The den grew warmer. After one full day, the egg moved. And then came a sharp, tapping sound.

The sorcerer sprang from his chair. A dark crack marked the huge egg's shell. As he watched, the crack lengthened and broadened, and at last the egg split in two.

But the creature that crawled out — a strange, naked

. . . an egg, lying in a nest of stones.

creature with stubby wings, a long, awkward neck, and a beak that seemed far too big for its body — was no dragon. It was some sort of bird.

Sick with disappointment and rage, the sorcerer raised his fist, intending to crush the life out of the miserable, squawking thing in the bowl.

Then something made him hesitate. Perhaps it was the way the bird's beak snapped closed like a trap. Perhaps it was its cruel talons, scrabbling on the surface of the bowl. Or perhaps it was just the cold, clear thought that if he could not have a dragon, then perhaps he should make do with what he had—at least for now.

Certainly it was not pity that made him lower his hand. And it was not pity that made him fetch raw meat, tear it into bloody strips, and watch the creature feed.

He knew that this creature was not native to the Land of Dragons. His servants had told him of every bird and beast they knew, and none of the birds they had described was like this one. Almost certainly its mother had been brought in a boat from a foreign land, then escaped to lay this egg on the mountaintop.

And he had found it, on the eve of his first triumph. He could see by the way it tore its meat that it could be trained to kill. He could see by the size of its beak and claws that it would grow to be very large.

The children of its flesh would be larger still — larger, stronger, and more savage. When he had finished his dread work, they would have teeth, and spines, and endless cunning. And they would be his devoted servants, killing and destroying at his command.

The work would take time and space. But soon he would have all the space he desired. And what was time, when in the end his will would triumph?

The sorcerer rubbed his bloodstained hands. His eyes shone red in the firelight as he made his plans.

The Tale of the Pirran Pipe

A TENNA BIRDSONG TALE

ong, long ago, beyond the mountains, there was a green land called Pirra, where the breezes breathed magic. Jealous shadows lurked on Pirra's borders, but the land was protected by a mysterious Pipe, which played notes of such beauty that no evil could take root within sound of its voice.

The Pipe was played morning, noon, and evening by the people's chief, the Piper, who was the finest player in the land.

One dark winter's night, the Piper of those days passed away in her sleep. The next day, three great musicians offered themselves as her replacement. They were called Plume the Brave, Auron the Fair, and Keras the Unknown.

The three played in turn before the people, as was the custom. Plume's playing was so stirring that the crowd cheered. Auron's music was so beautiful that her audience wept. Keras created sounds so haunting that all who heard them were rapt in wonder.

When the people voted to choose their favorite, each player received an equal number of votes. The three played again and again. But each time the result was the same.

Night fell, but the testing went on. The people, who had by now separated into three groups according to their favorite, grew tired and angry. But each person wanted his or her own choice to become Piper, and would not vote for another.

At last, long after midnight, when the vote was called equal for the thirteenth time, the three groups turned furiously upon one another, using their magic to insult and injure.

A man in a hooded cloak stepped forward. He was tall, but bent with weakness, as though the long day and night of music had been almost beyond his endurance. Each section of the crowd thought that he was one of its own, for he had spent time with all three, urging its members to hold firm.

"I have a solution, my friends!" he cried. "Let the contestants *share* the honor of being Piper. The Pipe is made from three parts that fit together. Let Plume, Auron, and Keras each take one part of the whole."

And so tired, so angry had the people become that they agreed. They gave Plume the mouthpiece of the Pipe, Auron the middle stem, and Keras the end piece. Then, because they still had bad feelings for one another, the three groups went their separate ways, each group following its own favorite.

The hooded man rubbed his hands, well satisfied, and slipped away like a shadow before the rising of the sun.

The dawn broke with no sound of music and the long day passed in silence, for the three rival groups were far apart, and no one piece of the Pirran Pipe could play alone.

Shadows crept into Pirra. Trees withered in their shade, and flowers wilted. Little by little the shadows swallowed up the green fields, the pleasant villages, while every moment the dread power cloaked within them grew stronger.

Long, long ago . . . there was a green land called Pirra.

Too late, the three groups realized their danger. Shadows now rolled dark between them. They could not reach one another to make the magic Pipe whole. And at last, seeing that their land was lost, they were forced to use the last of their magic to escape and save themselves.

So it was that the green land of Pirra became the Shadowlands. Its people, still blaming one another for their ancient loss, dwell to this day on three separate islands in a strange and secret sea.

And the Pirran Pipe, forever divided, is heard no more.

The Seven Goblins

Once upon a time, in hills to the south of the Land of Dragons, seven creatures climbed up from the underworld and stood upon the earth. They found that they had emerged into a great cave. The cave smelled of danger, and no wonder, for it was a dragon's den.

If the dragon had been at home, and hungry, this tale might have ended at once. But the dragon was out hunting, and the cave was empty.

With all speed, the seven creatures crawled out of the cave into a tall forest that was lit by the rising sun. Only the vine-weaver birds in the trees saw them coming.

The seven creatures wore garments as red as blood and carried packs upon their backs. Their skins were as pale as the skins of things that live beneath stones. Their eyes blinked and watered. They had the bodies of small humans, but their faces were like the faces of dogs.

The birds had never seen creatures like them and wondered who and what they were.

The seven creatures whispered together, looking here and there. Then they glanced behind them, as though they feared they were pursued. One, the largest of all, clutched his chest, as though beneath his clothes he carried something precious, something he should not have.

"Our quest is honorable," he said in a ringing voice. "We will survive. We will tell our story. We will find our people their place in the sun."

"Yes," agreed his companions. But fear and guilt twisted their faces, showing that they were not sure.

Just then, a man came creeping to drink at the pool that lay before the dragon's den. His name was Ben Os-Mine. His hair was wild and his beard was long. His clothes hung in rags about him. He had lived alone in the hills for many a long year, and the birds knew him well.

Ben Os-Mine visited the pool each day at sunrise, when he knew the dragon would be away from its den. On this morning he was to go thirsty. He saw the seven creatures who had come from the underworld and screamed in horror and disgust. The creatures drew back from him, snarling and pulling bone knives from their belts.

"Goblins!" Ben Os-Mine cried. And so the birds knew how to name the seven creatures, and called them "goblins" from that moment.

Ben Os-Mine seized a stone from a bag that hung from his belt. With the ease of long practice, for the hills were dangerous, he threw the stone hard and straight. It hit the smallest goblin in the center of her brow. Her heart stopped beating, and she fell dead upon the ground.

Her companions leaped forward, their weapons raised. But Ben Os-Mine turned and ran, and in moments he had disappeared into the darkness of the forest.

The goblins knelt, grieving, by their dead companion.

"The beings of this place are as ugly and as savage as we were told," one said at last. "Now we are only six. Perhaps we should turn back."

"There can be no turning back now," the large one answered grimly. "We made our decision, and must abide by it."

So the goblins buried their slain companion in a

shallow grave and left that place. They threaded their way through the tall trees until they reached the end of the forest's shade. Then harsh rocks tore their tender feet, and the bright sun hurt their eyes and burned their pale skin. But they bound grass and leaves around their feet and pulled hoods over their heads. And they stumbled on in a ragged line, their bone knives in their hands.

High above them, many dragons soared on the wind. The goblins did not notice them, for though the dragons' backs were gold as the sun, their undersides were palest blue, to match the sky.

The dragons saw the goblins and sensed that these red-cloaked strangers were both of their land, and not of it. They were curious, but did not bother to come to land. The wind was cool and pleasant beneath their wings. And, besides, they had breakfasted well already.

Many other eyes watched the goblins as they passed. The sharpest of these gleamed hungrily from stinking dens beneath the rocks and followed the strangers through secret passageways. The followers kept well hidden, for the points of the six bone knives shone in the sunlight, and the sky was filled with dragons.

But there came a time when the last goblin in line began to lag behind. The watching eyes brightened, waiting. At midday the last goblin fell exhausted to his knees, and his knife dropped from his hand.

Quick as a flash, a hairy arm reached from beneath a rock. Fingers like wires grasped the goblin's feet and dragged him down.

The other goblins swung around as their friend screamed. They saw that he had gone, and they rushed back to the place where he had been. But by the time they reached it the screams had stopped, and the silence was broken only by hideous, gobbling sounds.

"The fingers and toes were by far the sweetest," a

harsh voice cackled, from deep within the rock.

"They are always the sweetest," said another voice. "If I had my choice I would eat nothing else."

"Look what the creature had in his pocket," a third voice put in. "A cunning puzzle box. We should have made him show us how to open it."

"Too late now," the first voice growled. "We will make our next meal show us before it dies. Now, let me eat in peace. There is still meat on this bone."

Cold with horror, the five remaining goblins ran.

They ran until they had reached the end of the hills, then stumbled down to a grassy plain beyond. Darkness was falling, but still they forced themselves to continue, for they could see distant lights ahead.

They reached a lonely farmhouse and looked through its glowing window. A pot of soup bubbled on a black iron stove. A woman dozed in a chair. A little child played with wooden toys on a rug at her feet.

"These beings are hideous to look upon, but they do not seem savage," the largest goblin whispered. "We will make them listen to our story."

So he tap-tap-tapped at the window.

The child looked up from his play, saw the goblins' faces, and screamed. The woman jumped up in fright. Then she, too, saw the goblins. With a cry she seized the pot of soup from the stove and threw it at the window with all her might.

The heavy pot crashed through the glass. Four goblins sprang aside, but the fifth had paused an instant to draw his blade, and was too slow. Boiling soup poured over him, burning his tender flesh. Howling, he fell to the ground, and his heart was pierced by his own bone knife.

The woman and the child were screaming, screaming, screaming. The four goblins left alive heard hoarse shouts and the sound of heavy feet pounding towards the farm-

"Look what the creature had in his pocket."

house from a field beyond. They knew that another enemy was coming.

They fled, leaving their fallen companion where he lay.

For weeks they prowled the south, keeping hidden by day and traveling by night. Whenever they came to a house they peered into the windows and rattled the doors. But no one would let them in, and fear followed them wherever they went.

At last they reached a great town by the sea. Ships of many lands lay in the bay. There was much buying and selling in the market square, and plentiful talk and gossip, too.

Hidden in dark corners, skulking in foul-smelling alleyways, the goblins heard news of trouble in the far north — of attacks by bandit hordes and fearsome creatures who were said to be controlled by some dark power beyond the mountains.

Those tales were lightly told. The people of the south cared nothing, it seemed, for the troubles of the north. Stories of goblins terrorizing the countryside around the town were a different matter, however. When men and women spoke of these, their faces darkened, and they gathered their children close around them.

The goblins thought it best to be gone. They, too, had a tale to tell. But they had by now lost hope that they would ever tell it in this crowded, fearful town.

"We will go to the west," the leader said. "Have we not heard the savages in this town chatter of a magic city there? Surely the people of such a city will listen to us."

They spent an hour gathering food by creeping into sleeping houses. The hungriest among them found a tray of raisins on a pantry floor. Gleefully, she ate her fill, then tipped what remained into her food bag, thinking that her friends would never know of her greed.

But the raisins were poisoned, set out by the owner of

the house to kill rats. The goblin lived just long enough to warn her friends, then died horribly in their arms.

Under cover of darkness, the three remaining goblins fled the town and traveled west. For weeks they wandered, stealing scraps of food to live and sleeping in wretched holes. Their garments were thin rags. Their minds were filled with rage and pain.

At last the weakest of them died of hunger, cold and broken-hearted. The two remaining buried her, and went on, though by now they hardly knew why.

One day, at dawn, they saw a bright green field beside the road. Faint with hunger, the smaller of the two goblins staggered into the field.

He had hoped to eat of the flat, broad-leaved plants growing there. Instead, the plants ate him. The moment he touched one, jaws opened in its center and his arm was swallowed whole. In seconds he was sucked, screaming, into the plant's gaping throat, and was gone.

Now only one goblin remained — the largest of all, the leader, the one who carried stolen treasure around his neck. He was alone. His dreams were shattered, his anger had drained away. He did not even feel grief. Now all he wished to do was hide.

He ran through the rays of the rising sun until he came to a house with a broken roof and a door that swung wide. The goblin ran towards it. He crept through the open doorway, and looked around.

This house was dark and surely deserted, for it was foul with stinking, half-chewed bones, and everything was thick with dust. Just to be completely safe, however, the last goblin crawled beneath the sagging bed. *Here is a hiding place I can be sure of,* he said to himself.

But later that night, when he was fast asleep, the owner of that house came back.

The owner was a knight, the head of his clan. He had

been away for months on a raid and had celebrated his homecoming with two days and nights of feasting and a flood of ale.

He stamped into his dark, neglected house and flung himself upon the bed. The rotten timbers cracked under his weight and fell. The knight cursed but did not move. In moments he was snoring.

He slept till noon the following day and woke with a sore head amid the ruins of his bed. Grumbling, he rose and began to clear the wreckage away.

And there beneath the broken timbers was the crushed and lifeless body of the last goblin.

The knight stared, astonished. He knew what the dead thing was, for, as he said later, who but a goblin could be so hideous? He saw that the goblin's hands were clutched tightly together over his chest. He pried the dead fingers apart and found a bloodstained bag which held a small, carved piece of wood.

This must be a goblin talisman, he said to himself. *The goblin carried it around his neck for protection, no doubt. Well, it did not help him much! But surely it will help me. The talisman of a goblin I have killed — now, that is a lucky charm indeed!*

So he took the bloodstained bag and hung it around his own thick neck. Then he slung the goblin's body over his shoulder and went out to boast of yet another brave deed. For he saw no reason to tell a soul that he had killed the goblin by mistake. Why spoil a good story with the truth?

And so it was that the seven goblins never found their place in the sun. The few of their kind who followed later were no more fortunate. So not one soul in the Land of Dragons ever knew them, and no one ever heard the tale they had to tell.

Opal the Dreamer

A TENNA BIRDSONG TALE

On a plain in the heart of the Land of Dragons, beside a broad river, there once lived two simple, hardworking farmers named Liza and Dodd. Their farm was thick with apple trees, and they owned an old cart and a small herd of the three-legged beasts called muddlets. Now and then they would harness a muddlet to the cart and take a load of small, sweet apples across the plain to sell in the market of the nearby town.

They were not rich, but they were grateful for what they had. Their only sadness was that they had not been blessed with a child. They did not discuss this, however. They were people who thought it best not to speak of troubles that could not be helped.

One day, while Dodd was digging a new well, his spade struck rock and he saw bright colors flashing in the sun. With joy he realized that he had found a seam of precious stones. The stones were small cousins to his tribe's talisman, the huge, many-colored gem that was displayed in the great meeting hall of the town.

He ran to his wife, shouting that their fortunes had changed. And so it proved. Soon Liza and Dodd were making a good living by carving the rainbow stones from the rock. They would polish the stones until the colors shone like fire, then sell them to makers of rings, necklaces, and bracelets in the town.

Their lives became more comfortable. Then, to make their happiness complete, their dearest wish was granted. Twelve months to the day after Dodd made his discovery, a daughter was born to them.

Liza and Dodd could not believe their good fortune. They named their child Opal, in honor of the gems that had been the earth's gift, and swore to protect her from all harm.

They knew that they must continue working as hard as ever so their child could have all the comforts of life. They resolved, however, that Opal would not be left unguarded for a single moment.

For perils were everywhere on the Plains. Dragons were thick in the sky. Deadly scorpions lurked in the earth. Fighting spiders crouched beneath the rocks. Fierce bees swarmed in the apple trees. And the deep river ran swiftly.

So their workroom became Opal's nursery. From her birth, she lived in a world of gems that glittered with every color of the rainbow.

To Liza and Dodd, the stones were simply valuable objects that were helping to make them rich. To Opal, the stones were magic treasures, shining like the rainbow dragons that flew over the river.

Liza and Dodd would not let her touch the smallest, for fear she would put them in her mouth and choke. But they gave her the largest, and these she played with by the hour, caring little for other toys.

Her parents let her be. It pleased them to watch her baby games, and to hear her crooning to the stones as she played.

In the same way, they listened with smiles as Opal babbled of her dreams, though some of the things she

Perils were everywhere on the plain.

said made them both secretly uneasy. She had never left the farm in all her short life, yet her dreams were often of strange beasts and places — and events that plainly she did not understand. And sometimes she described things that her parents later discovered had come to pass.

Her words were the simple, stumbling words of a little child, however, and Liza and Dodd put their doubts aside. They told themselves that Opal had a lively imagination, and that it was only chance that made her dreams seem to predict the future.

Then, one morning when Opal was five years old, she chattered of a dream in which a man with a short white beard lay still beneath swift-running water. The man, she said, was staring up at the sky. One of his eyes was brown, and the other was blue.

Her parents glanced at each other. The man Opal had described was an important jeweler in the town. He was to come to the farm the very next day, to choose some special gems for a lady's necklace. But Opal had never seen him.

The next day, the jeweler did not come when he was expected. Dodd went out to look for him. He found the man drowned in the river, his dead, odd-colored eyes staring up at the sky, just as Opal had described.

Dodd was very afraid. He left the drowned man where he lay and ran to tell his wife.

Opal saw her parents whispering together, glancing at her now and then. She saw the fear in their faces, and grew afraid herself. When her father sternly ordered her never to tell anyone of her dream — never, indeed, to tell anyone her dreams anymore, she nodded and promised. When grave-faced men and weeping women came to take the dead man away in a cart, she watched from the house in silence.

She knew that somehow she had done a bad thing

by dreaming of the man in the river. She reasoned, in her childish way, that her dream had caused the man to die.

After that, Opal told her parents no more of her dreams. She did not want to make them angry. She wanted them to love her as they once did and to stop watching her as if they feared her.

But keeping silent about the dreams did not make them stop. Indeed, now that Opal could not tell her dreams freely, they seemed to come more often. Some she still did not understand, but those that were about her own place always came true.

If she dreamed the red cow would die, then it would happen. If she dreamed her mother would cut herself on the kitchen knife, it would be so. If she dreamed a dragon would carry off a baby muddlet, she knew that baby was doomed.

She said nothing to her parents, but she was too young to mask her face. They could always tell when she had dreamed of something that had come to pass. The dread in their eyes was terrible for Opal to see. Their silence weighed her down like a stone.

She sometimes woke, screaming, in the night, babbling of a wasteland beyond the mountains, of gray men who were not men, of terrible flying beasts, and of red eyes burning with hate. She babbled, too, of a man who could fight the Enemy — a man of iron and fire, who wore a band of bright stones around his waist.

Her nightmares roused the house. Her mother soothed her and wept. Her father cursed and pounded his fist against the wall. But they never spoke of it in the morning.

As Opal grew older she was no longer happy to remain in the workroom all day. She grew pale and fretful, and even her rainbow playthings did not comfort her. Liza and Dodd knew they had to allow her to wander the farm alone. But still they did all they could to keep her from harm.

To protect her from nesting dragons, they tied up her long black hair and hid it beneath a scarf. To protect her from scorpions and spiders they hid her feet in heavy leather boots, and her hands in hard leather gloves. To protect her from bees, they hid her face with a veil. To protect her from her own kind, they hid Opal herself. They forbade her to leave the farm and made it known that they did not welcome visitors.

They feared that if she mixed with others she might thoughtlessly betray her secret. They feared that simple folk might call her a witch and try to do her harm. They feared that the people of the town would turn against them, and no longer buy the gems that were making them rich.

They did not explain this to Opal. How could they, when they had never admitted to her that she had a gift at all? So she believed she was kept hidden because she was a monster who caused disaster by her dreams.

And so she grew in loneliness, trudging around the farm in her heavy boots, gazing at the broad river through her veil, and speaking freely only to the fish, the birds, and the bees. She did everything her parents wished, but she was angry and she feared to sleep, lest she dream they died, or the farmhouse burned to the ground.

At last there came a time when Opal was old enough to realize that her dreams did not *make* the future, but merely foretold it. She felt a vast relief. But that night she had a nightmare worse than any she had ever known.

She saw the gray men that were not men swarming across the distant mountains from the shadows beyond. She saw a pack of foul, winged beasts attack a rainbow dragon above the broad river. She saw a city lying in ruins, and a great evil dwelling within its walls. She saw a hooded figure, and red eyes burning with hatred.

She saw salvation — strong arms beating white-hot steel, and seven spaces in the steel, waiting to be filled.

She woke with a beating heart, knowing that what she saw would come to pass. She ran to Liza and Dodd and woke them. She told them of what she had seen. She begged them to warn the people — before it was too late.

Liza and Dodd shook their heads and put their hands over their ears. They ordered her to be silent, for her own sake and theirs.

But Opal had had enough of silence. She ran from the house, her long hair streaming behind her, black as the night sky.

Her bare feet touched the earth for the first time as she ran across the Plains. For the first time she felt the cool air full on her face and saw the moon and the stars above her with unveiled eyes. She laughed and cried together. And as dawn broke she ran through the gates of the town and into the great meeting hall where the tribe's talisman was kept.

The townspeople woke to her shrill cries of warning. They tumbled out of their beds and flocked to the great hall. They saw a slim, barefoot girl in a long white nightgown, standing by the rainbow gem on its pedestal of silver.

The girl's black hair hung, tangling, to her waist. Her soft hand rested on the talisman, as if she drew courage from its fiery light. She called out that the people must prepare for battle with the Lord of Shadows behind the mountains.

The people laughed or turned away in pity, thinking that Opal was a poor soul who had lost her wits. Most had heard of the troubles in the north, and they were all of the same opinion.

What harm could a few raiding parties from across the mountains do? The real enemies of the Plains tribe had always been the savage people to the west, and the tribe of brutish warriors in the south.

"Listen to me!" cried Opal, stretching out her hands. "The danger is real. I have dreamed it, and my dreams do not lie. But there is hope. One day, a man of iron and fire will come. You must do what this man bids you and give him whatever he asks. But while you wait for him, you must beware. The eyes of the Lord of Shadows are upon our land. His monsters are coming to destroy us!"

But the people smiled, went about their business, and did not listen to what she said.

Opal's parents came to take her home, but she shook her head and would not move. Three times they came. Then, despairing, they left her, and her name was not spoken between them ever again.

Day after day Opal stood in the great hall, vainly calling out her message. Kind folk brought her food and drink, warm clothes, and shoes for her feet. She thanked them and carried on with the work she had resolved to do.

Days became weeks. Weeks became months. Still Opal stood beside the tribe's talisman in the great hall, calling out her message. And still no one listened.

One night, exactly a year after her arrival in the town, Opal dreamed again of the man of iron and fire. The next morning, the townspeople woke to find that she was gone.

Many were sorry. They had grown used to her presence among them. They had not listened to her, but now they missed her. They spoke of her to one another, wondering why she had left them.

Opal had gone to find the man in her dream. Great fish had carried her across the broad river. Now she was moving south, away from the plains of her birth.

She told everyone she met along the way of the danger growing in strength beyond the mountains. No one paid attention to her words, but no one troubled her, either, for a swarm of bees flew around her head, guarding her from all harm. After a time, she came to another river, and followed it until she reached the sea. There she found a town even larger than the one she had left.

She walked through the town, and the people stared. She walked until she came to a place where a great fire burned, and a blacksmith hammered red-hot iron. And there the bees left her and flew back to their own place, for they had done their part.

Opal stepped into the forge. The blacksmith turned to look at her. She realized at once that he was not the man she sought. The man in her dream had not yet been born. She knew that now.

But this man's face was kind, and his arms were strong. She understood that he was her destiny.

And so she stayed with him. She told him of her dreams, and he listened as no one else had ever done.

But now that she was away from the place of her birth, the dreams were coming less often. By the time she and the blacksmith were married, they had stopped altogether. By the time her first child was born, her early life itself had begun to seem like a dream.

Time passed, and years became tens of years. On the farm by the river, Dodd and Liza grew old, then died. Their house decayed, and their money box rusted. Dust filled their mine of rainbow stones. Their muddlet herd ran wild. The fierce bees swarmed in the apple trees, waiting for another strong enough to command them.

The town of the Plains grew and became a city. Sometimes, at night, old ones still told tales of the poor, mad girl who had once cried warnings in the great hall. But the tales of these old ones were soon forgotten. And after a time, there was no one left to remember Opal the Dreamer, or to wonder what had become of her.

And there was no one left to remember her dreams.

The Shadow Army

RETOLD FROM *THE DELTORA ANNALS*

As years went by, the northern tribes of the Land of Dragons grew accustomed to battling sudden, fierce raids from the place beyond the mountains. They began to call this place the Shadowlands, for its borders were cloaked in darkness. No one had ever seen it and returned to tell the tale.

The people learned that the desperate raiders who swooped down on their villages were branded like beasts with the sign of a hand. They learned that these wild-eyed, branded souls preferred death to defeat, for the one they called their master did not forgive failure.

They learned, too, that the prime aim of the raids was to take prisoners. They shuddered as they wondered what fate awaited those wretched men, women, and children dragged away in chains.

And so it went on, for so long that the raids began to seem part of everyday life in the north. Few suspected that a terrible plan was being put into action, and the Enemy in the Shadowlands was growing stronger day by day.

But there came a time when the Land of Dragons felt the true rage and jealousy of the power in the Shadowlands. There came a time when red clouds boiled behind the mountains, and a great army streamed through the pass of the northwest, killing and burning every living thing in its path.

All who first saw that army cried out in horror, for though its leaders were human, its soldiers were ghastly, shambling creatures, like clumsy figures of clay or dough that a young child might make in play. And above the hordes flew seven monstrous, vulturelike birds the likes of which the tribes of the north had never seen.

At first, these birds were called dragon birds. Later, when the people of the coast saw them, they became known as the seven Ak-Baba, for they resembled fearsome birds of that name seen by sailors in distant ports.

But the seven were plainly not wild birds. They were far larger than the birds the sailors had seen. They had teeth and spines, and a foul odor hung about them. They had been bred to kill and seemed to obey orders no one else could hear, as if their minds were linked with the mind of their master beyond the mountains.

The people of the north fought valiantly. The dragons of the north fought also, battling the Ak-Baba and cutting great swathes through the army, swooping from the air with fire gusting from their jaws.

The Ak-Baba worked as a pack, slaughtering dragons where they could, fleeing back to the mountains and safety when the dragons were too many to defeat. They were wily, and no weapon seemed to harm them.

It was soon clear, however, that the gruesome-looking soldiers could die like other mortals. They were slain in their thousands, despite their helmets and breastplates, but as they died, thousands more took their places.

The people of the north began to call them the Greers, after certain grunting sounds they made, and they were soon known by this name throughout the land. Though they were clumsy and stupid in battle, they were terrifying foes, for they were many, their cruelty was boundless, and senseless violence was meat and drink to them.

They did not know the meaning of retreat. They would clamber over piles of their fallen comrades to battle an enemy. They cared no more for their own safety than did the fighting spiders of the Plains, and even their commanders seemed to fear them.

The army spread its ranks along the mountains from west to east and began pressing on towards the south. It overwhelmed everything in its path, because the tribes of the Land of Dragons were still strictly divided, and singly no tribe could repel the invader.

One by one, the tribes with northern borders — the gnomes of Dread Mountain, and the people of the Mere, the Plains, and Ralad — were forced to abandon the countryside of their territories. They fell back to their towns and cities, which could be better defended. But if the invading army could not subdue a town in its path, it went around it, always moving south as if determined to cover the whole land with its shadow.

News moved slowly in the Land of Dragons in those days, for neighboring tribes rarely shared talk or trade. Desperate folk fleeing certain death do not care for borders, however. Soon ragged souls were streaming into the southern territories of Del and the Jalis, seeking refuge and warning of the terror to come.

In their city of Jaliad, the Jalis prepared for war with relish. They listened in contempt to the babbling of the wretched folk who dared to cross their borders, then killed them without mercy. They told one another that the invaders might find other tribes easy prey, but would think again when they faced the warrior Jalis.

The Jalis had not seen the Shadow Army, but they could not imagine a force their tribe could not defeat. Their talisman was the diamond, gem of strength, and they had never been beaten in any fight. So they sharpened their

The Ak-Baba worked as a pack . . .

weapons and reveled in a merry feast, looking forward to the glorious battle to come.

In the city of Del to the east, however, the case was very different. Del was a bustling place, the largest city in the land and a great seaport. It was a city used to strangers and strange ideas, a city of buying and selling, where rumors spread like wildfire.

The strongest troops marched out of the city to defend the borders of the Del tribe's territory. Great crowds lined the streets to cheer them on their way, but no one felt safe. Every day there was more frightful news of slaughter in the north. Foreign traders hurriedly set sail for home, and terror gripped the city.

Then, as suddenly as it had begun, the invasion faltered. Winter had come — a hard, cold winter, too. Intent on advancing at all costs and utterly careless of their lives, the Greers froze to death in huge numbers.

They were by now too far from the mountains for replacements to be sent with speed. The Shadow Army's numbers fell rapidly, and its ambitious commanders were forced to halt its progress.

The people of Del thanked the heavens they had been spared. A few chose to believe that their tribe's talisman, the great topaz, had saved them, for it was the gem of faith. Wiser souls knew that safety would last only as long as the winter chill, and they continued to prepare for war.

These wiser ones knew that their lives had changed forever. The Enemy in the Shadowlands at last revealed his power and his will. He had sent the creatures of his sorcery to take the Land of Dragons in his name, and he would not be content till all of it was his.

Only a miracle could defeat the being they had begun to call the Shadow Lord.

Adin the Blacksmith

RETOLD FROM *THE DELTORA ANNALS*

n the city of Del, at the time of the Shadow Army's invasion, there lived a man named Adin. Adin was a blacksmith, a maker of swords and armor and shoes for horses. He was well liked among his neighbors, for he was a man of honesty and sense, and his ready laugh cheered all who heard it.

When the first news of the Shadow Army reached his ears, Adin grew at once more grave. While others were still gossiping lightheartedly of this new, outlandish tale from the north, Adin was deep in thought.

He had more reason than most to be troubled. As it happened, the news reminded him unpleasantly of scraps of family history he had heard by the fireside as a child.

His father, who had been the blacksmith before him, was a great storyteller and often told stories of the family that had been passed down through the generations. The young Adin had loved these tales of his ancestors, though it was hard to tell how much truth was in them.

There was the tale of Silas the Strong, a black-bearded giant of a man who first built the forge in Del.

There was the tale of Silas's great-granddaughter, Sophie, who had found a dead goblin in the backstreets of Del, when she was nine years old.

There was the tale of Primus, the ancestor who was killed by the Jalis in a fierce border war.

There was the tale of the great-great-uncle who, at sixteen, argued with his parents, ran away to the Forests of Silence, and was never seen again.

And there was the tale of the ancestor called Opal the Dreamer, who had claimed to have the gift of prophecy.

It was said that Opal was beautiful, but very strange. It was said that she had come from the land of the Plains in a swarm of bees. It was said that when each of her seven sons was born, and was put into her arms, she would look searchingly into his eyes and sigh, "No, thank the heavens, little man. You are not the one. The time of terror is still to come."

It was said that she later did the same with her grandsons, and her great-grandsons, too, and died at a great age, still waiting, it seemed, for the boy child she half feared, half longed to see.

The story concentrated on Opal's strangeness. Little was said of her prophecies. All that was remembered of them was that one day monsters and men who were not men would be sent by the Lord of Shadows beyond the mountains to conquer the Land of Dragons.

Adin's family had never chattered to outsiders of Opal the Dreamer. A Plains ancestor, and one with such strange ways, too, was not something to be proud of in Del. But in the family circle, by the fireside, Opal *was* spoken of now and then. Adin was not the first child of his clan whose imagination had been captured by her strange, unfinished story.

Now, it seemed, Opal's visions were coming true. Adin tried not to believe it, but the more he heard from the north, the more convinced of it he became. The Greers were clearly men who were not men. The dragon birds were monsters. And both had been sent by the power beyond the mountains.

Did this mean that what Opal had called "the time of doom" was near? If it did, what of the man she had been waiting for? Who and where was he?

Is it possible that I am the one? Adin thought unwillingly. Roughly, he pushed the question away, but it stole back, uninvited. *Was* he the descendant Opal had awaited? If so, what was expected of him? What part was he to play?

To drive these troubling thoughts away, he began working harder than ever before. He no longer practiced the archery that once he had loved. He no longer joined his friends in the tavern as darkness fell or read by the fireside at night. It became common for him to labor in the forge till midnight, then rise again with the dawn to work again.

But no matter how hard he worked, a shadow hung over him. Questions plagued him and disturbed his rest. He could not eat. He no longer took pleasure in the small things that had once brought him comfort.

One night, when the moon was full, he stumbled into his dark house, kicked off his boots, and threw himself exhausted onto his bed. He fell at once into a deep sleep. And he dreamed.

He dreamed of a belt — a splendid belt made of steel beaten to the thinness of silk. The belt had seven medallions linked together by fine chain. In each of the medallions was a huge gem, shining like fire.

One gem was a diamond, sparkling like ice. One was a ruby, red as blood. One was an amethyst, purple as the violets that grew on the banks of the River Del. One was an emerald, green as lush grass. One was like the night sky — dark blue pierced with points of light. One flashed with every color of the rainbow.

And one was golden as the sun. In wonder, Adin

recognized it as the great topaz, the Del tribe's ancient talisman, which now lay in a glass case in the city's meeting hall. And somehow, in his dream, he came to understand that the other gems in the belt were talismans also — the talismans of the other six tribes of the Land of Dragons.

The belt was as clear as day to him. He could see it in every detail. And he knew that his own hands had made it.

Adin woke, sweating and trembling. The light of the moon was streaming through the window, shining full on his face. The picture of the belt was burning in his brain.

Then, suddenly, a great calm descended on his troubled mind. Suddenly, he knew what he had to do.

He rose from his rumpled bed and pulled on his boots. He splashed cold water on his face. He made tea and drank it hot and steaming. He ate heartily of bread and cheese. Then he strode out to the forge, beneath the moon, and began at once to create the belt he had seen in his dream.

That night was only the beginning. For many nights following he labored in secret. He needed no plans, for the design was as clear in his mind as if it had been drawn there with pen and ink. And when the work was finished at last he knew he had done well.

The belt was the finest thing he had ever made. He could hardly believe that his own hands had fashioned it, though he was a master of his trade. Even plain and unadorned, it was beautiful.

He allowed himself to enjoy it for one full night. Then he put it aside and set to work again, making himself the strongest sword he could fashion, and arrowheads enough to serve him for a long and perilous journey.

For such a journey was ahead of him now, and it had to begin soon. Adin knew that the medallions in the belt had to be filled. He knew he was the one who must fill them.

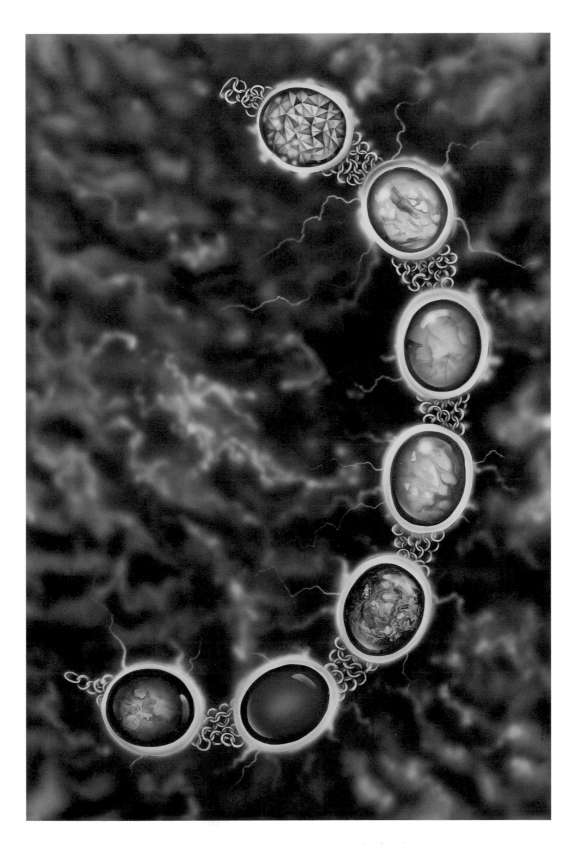

He dreamed of a belt—a splendid belt made of steel . . .

And he knew that he could not begin his quest in Del.

In Del, he was well known. He had grown to manhood there — a familiar face in the tavern and the marketplace as well as at the forge.

Some might think that this would make his task easier, but Adin knew it would not. He was too wise to hope that his own people would respect him as they would respect a stranger. If he spoke to them of a dream and a magic belt, if he asked them to give him the great topaz, they would merely laugh at him or pity him. They would whisper among themselves that Adin the blacksmith had lost his wits.

But if he came to them with other gems in the belt, and they saw with their own eyes that other tribes believed in him, the case might be very different.

When all was ready, Adin strode from the forge without looking back. His bow was on his shoulder, and his sword was near his hand. Around his waist was the dream belt, its seven empty medallions waiting to be filled.

It was just before the dawn. All Del lay silent, dark, and sleeping. And so it was that Adin the blacksmith left the city of his birth unnoticed by a soul, and set out to meet his destiny.

The Warrior Jalis

RETOLD FROM *THE DELTORA ANNALS*

din the blacksmith turned his face to the west and let his feet take him towards the land of the Jalis. It crossed his mind that certain death awaited him there, but he put the thought aside.

The Shadow Army had not yet reached the territory of the Jalis. It made good sense to start his quest there. And, besides, if the dream belt he wore was to be completed, the savage Jalis must be faced at last. So why not face them first, and let fate decide the rest?

So Adin told himself as he moved west. But, in truth, it was not his mind, but his heart, which was leading him. He did not know why the land of the Jalis was to be his first goal. He knew only that there he must go.

He crossed the Jalis border in darkness, and moved on without seeing a soul, which suited him very well. His aim was to reach the main town of Jaliad without being challenged. It seemed to him that he was more likely to get a hearing from the Jalis leaders than from the fierce folk in the countryside.

As dawn was breaking, he saw a small, dark hut on the outskirts of a village. The hut looked abandoned, so he approached it, thinking to use it as shelter for the day ahead. But no sooner had he put his hand upon the sagging door than the door flew open. There stood a knight in golden armor — a Jalis warrior, thirsting for a fight.

"Kneel, worm of Del!" roared the Jalis, raising his sword. "Prepare to die!"

"I have no wish to fight you, Jalis, but I must go my way," said Adin, drawing his own sword. "I must go to Jaliad, to speak to your leaders."

The knight bellowed with laughter. "Indeed?" he roared. "Then I will take them your ugly head, and it can speak for you."

With that, he lunged forward.

Adin was no great swordsman. He was far more skillful with a bow and arrow. But there was no time to change his weapon now, and he would not run. He met the attack head-on, and the sword he had made was so light, yet so strong, that he was able to turn the knight's huge weapon aside and make him stumble.

The knight recovered himself and laughed again.

"Aha!" he cried. "This worm has teeth! All the better! I long for a little sport!"

He attacked again, even more ferociously, but again Adin managed to turn the giant sword away and keep his head upon his shoulders.

With a roar, the knight began to fight in earnest. Desperately, Adin ducked and weaved, defending himself against the savage blows. Sometimes he even managed a thrust of his own, only to hear his sword clang uselessly against his foe's golden armor.

He was strong from a lifetime of wielding the great hammer of the forge. But the knight was stronger. Minute by minute Adin felt himself weakening, while the knight seemed as fresh as the moment the fight began.

At last, Adin's sword was knocked from his hand. The next moment he was flat on the ground, with the knight's

There stood a knight in golden armor . . .

boot on his neck and the point of the knight's sword pressed to his heart.

And so my quest ends before it has begun, Adin thought as he waited for death. But the Jalis put down a gold-gloved hand, and hauled him to his feet.

"You fight well, for a weakling," the knight said, pulling off his helmet to reveal his sweating, brutish face. "You have given me great sport. Tomorrow, I will kill you. Tonight, you feast with the Jalis."

He picked up the fallen sword, then dragged Adin around the corner of the hut, to where a cart and four strong horses stood waiting. He threw his prisoner into the back of the cart, amid a mess of bones, empty sacks, and giant pumpkins, and took the reins in his hands.

"My name is Greel," he said, grinning over his shoulder at Adin. "My clan is mighty, and blessed with good fortune. One of my ancestors killed a goblin in this very place. Around my neck I wear the goblin's talisman, passed down to me through the generations. It means I cannot die in battle, or so I have always been told."

He nodded, as if satisfied that his boasting had impressed his prisoner sufficiently. Then he shook the reins. The horses set off down the road at a great pace. And so it was that Adin, wondering at the strangeness of the Jalis, was carried like a sack of grain to Jaliad.

It was dark when they arrived in the town. Greel pulled Adin from the cart and swaggered with him into a hall, where a riotous feast was in progress.

The feasting hall was vast and low, lit with flaming torches and filled with smoke, heat, noise, and the mingled smells of unwashed bodies, fire, and cooking meat.

Whole beasts turned on spits at one end of the room. At the other end was a huge fireplace, set on a raised platform of stone. An ancient crone crouched in a chair by the blazing fire, smacking her lips over a steaming bowl.

The rest of the feasting hall was filled with many long tables loaded with platters of meat, bread, fruit, and vast jugs frothing with ale. Huge, roughly dressed men and women sat crowded along the benches, eating with their hands and knives. A great chair stood empty at the head of the longest table, close to the fire.

Greel shouted a greeting. Heads turned. A great roar went up, and hundreds of greasy fists punched the air in welcome. Greel led Adin to the head of the longest table and bellowed for another chair. Adin realized, astounded, that his captor must be someone of great importance. Perhaps, indeed, he was the leader of all his tribe!

"This puny worm of Del fights with the heart of a Jalis," Greel roared. "Let him be treated well, as befits a valiant foe on his last night alive!"

A platter of steaming, bloody meat topped with a great hunk of bread was slammed down in front of Adin. A beaker of ale was thrust into his hand.

Beside him, Greel threw aside his armored gloves and began to gorge, swilling ale straight from the jug, tearing meat from bones and throwing the bones to the floor.

"Eat! Drink!" he shouted at Adin.

Unwilling to anger him, Adin drank a little and ate what he could. But his head was swimming with the heat of the raging fire at his back, and the sight of the bloody meat made his stomach churn.

When Greel had eaten his fill, he belched loud and richly and pounded his fist on the table for silence.

"My prisoner has a tale to tell us, warriors of Jalis!" he roared. "Would you relish some entertainment? If his tale pleases us, we will set him free and let him run until we catch him. If it does not please us, we will have his head at once. What say you to that?"

The other Jalis laughed and bellowed agreement.

Greel took Adin by the front of his coat and hauled

him to his feet. Adin swayed, sick and dizzy, and clutched the table for support. His eyes watering in the room's smoky haze, he stared at the rows of red, grinning faces turned towards him. Dimly, he wondered what madness had made him think he could ever convince these people of anything.

"I am Adin, blacksmith of Del," he began, and he could hear his voice trembling.

"Speak up!" shrieked an enormous, bushy-haired woman at the end of the room. "Greel, your brave prisoner squeaks like a mouse!"

"What wonder is there in that?" jeered a man. "All men of Del are mice!"

The room shook with bellows of laughter.

Adin felt a flash of anger, and suddenly, his mind cleared.

If this is my last night on earth, then so be it, he thought, pushing himself upright. *By a miracle I have been given the chance I wished for, and I will take it.*

"I am Adin, blacksmith of Del!" he shouted. The noise in the room fell to a guffawing murmur and he went on, taking pleasure in the new strength of his voice. "I am not a warrior," he said loudly. "I am not a leader. I am an ordinary man who works with iron and fire. I have come to you, in peril of my life, because not long ago I had a dream, and I knew from the dream what I must do."

He realized to his surprise that the room had grown utterly still. The Jalis were all gaping at him, ragged bones held halfway to their mouths, beakers of ale hanging forgotten in their hands.

He pulled his coat aside, and showed them the steel belt he wore around his waist. He told them of his dream. Still the room was silent, except for the crackling of the fire.

He took a deep breath. "The belt waits to be filled

with the talismans of all the seven tribes," he said. "The gems must be united, and the tribes also, if the Lord of Shadows is to be defeated. I ask the brave Jalis, here and now, to be the first to offer their talisman to the cause."

He waited, breathless, for the cries of jeering anger he knew must come. He heard Greel breathing hard and braced himself for the blow that any moment would send him sprawling.

But no cries of anger rose, and no blow fell. Instead, Greel spoke, his growling voice trembling with some great emotion.

"You know little of our tribe, man of Del," Greel said. "I doubt you have ever heard the name Tenna of the Jalis."

"I have not heard it," Adin admitted in confusion. This was not the response he had expected. What did the Jalis mean by it?

"Tenna lived long ago," said Greel. "As a child, she found a blackbird caught in a net. She released the bird, and, in return, it told her many wondrous tales."

Adin glanced at him. No smile twitched upon Greel's lips. His small eyes were deadly serious.

Greel really believed this tale of a talking bird. And, looking around the room, Adin saw that all the other Jalis did, too. Again he wondered at the strangeness of these people, who killed ruthlessly on the one hand, and believed nursery tales on the other.

Yet I am asking them to believe in me, he reminded himself. He wondered if that was Greel's point. If he, Adin, could not believe in storytelling blackbirds, why should the Jalis believe in a stranger's dream? He waited tensely for what was to come.

"Tenna remembered the tales, word for word," Greel said. "It became the work of her life to tell them to others. They became known as the Tenna Birdsong Tales and have been treasured by the Jalis ever since. They are passed down from generation to generation, and the words never vary."

Adin nodded politely. His mind was racing. With his eyes he measured the distance between his chair and the other end of the room. He was standing, but the Jalis were all seated. Was it possible for him to reach the door without being caught? If he took them by surprise . . .

"Sit!" Greel ordered roughly. And Adin had no choice but to obey.

Greel gestured at the old crone sitting silently on the raised platform by the fire. "This is Tatti," he said. "Her years number one hundred and one. She is a direct descendant of Tenna and the present guardian of the Birdsong Tales. She is our greatest storyteller. Long may she live."

"Long may she live," the crowd echoed.

Adin bowed his head to the ancient woman. She made no movement in reply, but her faded eyes were fixed on him and her bony, spotted hands clutched the empty bowl on her lap so tightly that her knuckles were white.

"I now ask Tatti to tell us a tale," Greel said. "She knows which one I mean. Never has she told it, or any tale, before a stranger. But you must hear it, man of Del."

Adin bowed again, taking the opportunity to ease his chair a little farther from the table.

I will wait until the tale has begun, he thought. *I will wait until these childish savages are all enthralled by their storyteller. Then I will make my move.*

The old woman had not stirred. She was still staring at Adin, staring greedily, as if she could never have enough of the sight of him. Or perhaps she could read his mind, and knew what he was planning.

Adin felt a knot tightening in his chest as she opened her mouth to speak.

"This is a Tenna Birdsong Tale," the old woman said, and Adin caught his breath. The voice was deep, strong, and charged with a strange, throbbing excitement. It was almost shocking to hear it issuing from those withered lips.

The storyteller paused. The fire roared and spat. Adin moved, as if settling himself more comfortably. Now his feet were clear of both chair and table legs. One of his hands gripped the edge of the table; the other lay casually on the chair back.

I will thrust the chair at Greel when I run, he thought.

He glanced at the storyteller. Her eyes, gleaming in the firelight, caught and held him. He could not look away. She took a breath, and when she spoke again, though her voice filled the whole vast room, it was as if she was speaking only to him.

"The name of my tale," she said, "is 'Opal the Dreamer.'"

Adin's heart gave a mighty thud and his jaw fell open. He heard Greel grunt with satisfaction and knew the Jalis had been watching him, waiting for this moment.

The storyteller half smiled and began. "*On a plain in the heart of the Land of Dragons, beside a broad river, there once lived two simple, hardworking farmers named Liza and Dodd . . .*"

Her voice continued, and Adin sat still, enraptured and astonished, all thought of escape forgotten. He could hardly believe that in this vast, alien hall, filled with the people of a tribe he had feared and despised all his life, he was hearing his own ancestor's story, passed from a blackbird to a child long ago.

But it was true. In a daze he listened to the tale of Opal the Dreamer, and his face burned as he began to understand what it meant, why he had been led to this place, and what his coming meant to the Jalis.

"*She sometimes woke, screaming, in the night, babbling of a wasteland beyond the mountains, of gray men who were not men, of terrible flying beasts, and of red eyes burning with hate,"* crooned the storyteller, her voice low and throbbing, but reaching every corner of the room. *"She babbled, too, of a man who could fight the Enemy — a man of iron and fire, who wore a band of bright stones around his waist . . ."*

Adin felt the eyes of the room upon him. He saw the storyteller's ancient eyes widen, as if the words, said so often before, had taken on fresh meaning. As he put his hands to the empty belt, he was filled with awe.

The storyteller spoke on. Her eyes never left Adin's face, and he hung on her every word, spellbound.

At last he could tell by her voice, and by the feeling in the room, that the story was coming to a close.

"And after a time, there was no one left to remember Opal the Dreamer, or to wonder what had become of her," the old woman finished softly. *"And there was no one left to remember her dreams."*

She bowed her head. With a great scraping of benches, the Jalis stood, cheering and punching the air with their fists. Adin, too, stumbled to his feet. He had been sitting so still that his legs had grown numb.

The moment the cheering ended, Greel kicked his chair aside. Without a word, he climbed the stone platform and took a golden box from the shelf above the fire. He held the box high, showing it to the watching people.

"The fools of the Plains may have forgotten Opal the Dreamer, but the Jalis have not," he said. "Still, we have been in error. We have believed that the dread time she foretold was not yet upon us, for the man of iron and fire had not yet arisen. But now he is here, among us, and we know what we must do."

He opened the box and took from it a huge, glittering diamond. "Bring the belt forward," he said.

Adin removed the steel belt from his waist. He

climbed the shallow steps of the platform, and held the belt out to Greel.

Greel lowered the diamond into the first medallion, beside the clasp. The great gem slid smoothly into place.

"So, the first space in the belt is filled," said Greel. "And it is fitting that the Jalis diamond fills it. For the Jalis tribe is the first and greatest of all the seven tribes."

He raised his fist, and again the room shook with the sound of cheering and the stamping of feet. But the eyes of the Jalis were fixed longingly on their talisman as Adin fastened the belt once more around his waist.

"I will protect your treasure with my life," Adin said, finding his voice at last. "I will repay your trust in me, I swear it."

"The great diamond cannot be stolen without ill fortune following the thief," said Greel. "But we have given it to you freely, and it will bring you strength."

He raised his bushy eyebrows. "Nevertheless, you cannot leave us until I have given you some instruction in swordplay, Adin of Del. Your heart may be the heart of a warrior, and your sword is a fine one, but your skills are woeful. And the other tribes of this land cannot be trusted."

Adin did not argue with this speech. He had learned much during his time with the Jalis.

"Never could I hope to defend your talisman as well as a Jalis might do," he said quietly. "But I would greatly value your help, Greel, so I can do my best."

He held out his hand. Grinning broadly, Greel clasped it in both his own. And so, for the first time, a man of Del and a man of the Jalis touched in friendship instead of hatred.

It was but one small moment in a night to remember. But of such moments, great history is made.

The Dread Gnomes

RETOLD FROM *THE DELTORA ANNALS*

With the great diamond heavy in his dream belt, Adin the blacksmith left the land of the Jalis and entered the mysterious realm of Tora.

He entered it with high hopes. All he had heard of the ancient magic of Tora had convinced him that the Torans would readily understand the story of his dream.

Six tribes had still to be persuaded that unity was the land's only hope of salvation. Of them all, Adin was sure that the tribe of Tora would be the one to add its talisman to the belt most eagerly — and with most faith. Toran magic would surround him, then, and speed him on his way.

But no sooner had he crossed the border than he felt cold pain in his heart and mind. The Torans, enclosed in their white marble city, had felt a stranger's presence and were repelling him with magic.

Adin set his teeth against the pain, pressed his hand to the great diamond for strength, and moved on along the banks of the River Tor.

The farther he went, the more he saw the devastation left by the Shadow Army. No doubt the Greers had also felt the Toran pain, but it had not made them turn from their terrible work. Villages were burned. Boats were floating hulks in the cold, sluggish waters of the river.

But no Ak-Baba prowled the skies. No grunting Greers haunted the banks of the river. The Jalis had told him truly, it seemed. The Shadow Army had withdrawn to the center of the Land of Dragons, to wait through the cold months of winter.

The pain was growing stronger. Soon it was so strong that he could hardly breathe, hardly put one foot before the other. Then he saw the city of Tora ahead. The city stood whole, perfect, and untouched by strife. But when he tried to turn aside from his path to enter it, he could not.

He was unable to stop, unable even to pause, beside Tora's perfect, gleaming beauty. The power streaming from within the city repelled him as surely as it had repelled the Enemy. The power seized his legs and swept him on along the river, as helpless as dust before a broom — raging, but helpless to resist.

Soon the magic city was far behind him, and the mountains of the north were large on the horizon. Adin felt the pain leave him and knew he had crossed the Toran border into the territory of the Dread Gnomes.

The hulking shape of Dread Mountain loomed before him. Behind the mountain's peak, the sky of the Shadowlands swirled with scarlet cloud.

Adin had never seen a Dread Gnome, but the tales he had heard of the tribe were fearsome. Dread Gnomes were cruel and cunning, it was said, and they loved jewels and gold more than life itself. They were fiercely jealous of their territory, and hated all strangers.

These stories were far from comforting. And now Adin knew that his hopes of Toran protection had been false hopes. The Torans had turned their backs on him. Fate had decreed that Dread Mountain was to be his next goal and that he was to face it unprotected.

He took his sword in his hand and trudged on.

The rough road at the base of the mountain, and the foothills through which Adin began cautiously to climb, were covered in snow. And the snow was thick with the frozen, half-decayed bodies of Greers stuck full of arrows.

There were the bodies of strange, fearsome beasts, too — things like giant green lizards with great, clawed feet, snarling, needle-sharp teeth, and tiny orange eyes. But these creatures, too, were quite dead, crushed beneath vast rocks that must have come crashing down upon them from the slopes above.

There had been a mighty battle here — and terrible slaughter. The Gnomes of Dread Mountain had shown the Greers what it meant to be savage. Adin began to climb even more warily, sword in hand, alert to every sound.

He climbed for a long time, following a path that ran beside a frozen stream. Dark, thorny trees closed in about him. He heard nothing, nothing at all except the gurgling of the water beneath its shroud of ice.

The mountain seemed deserted — empty of every living thing. Yet now and then he came upon marks in the snow. Mostly these were the marks of small, booted feet. But sometimes they were the huge, deep prints of a heavy creature with three toes and massive claws.

Pictures of the smashed, scaly beasts he had seen at the foot of the mountain flickered in Adin's mind like warning lights. It seemed that at least one of the creatures was still alive and roaming the mountain.

But still he climbed. And still he saw nothing.

He stopped to rest. He sheathed his sword and bent his head to unscrew the cap of his water flask. And in that instant, he realized that he was no longer alone. When he looked up, a dozen short, stocky figures clothed in garments of smooth brown fur stood before him. Each figure held a drawn bow. A dozen arrows were aimed at his heart.

The arrows were only half the size of Adin's, but he knew that any one of them would be more than enough to kill a man, if it was aimed true. And the Dread Gnomes' skill with their bows was legendary.

Slowly, Adin looked around. More menacing figures stood on either side of him. By the prickling on the back of his neck he knew there were still more behind.

"I come in peace," he said, holding out his hands. "Do not harm me."

But even as he spoke he wondered why he was not already dead. The Gnomes' eyes were glittering with dislike. The bowstrings were straining in their hands.

"Drop your weapons, stranger," one of them said sharply. It was a harsh, female voice, and the voice of a leader.

Slowly, Adin took his bow from his shoulder and put it at his feet. Then he unbuckled his sword and let it fall to the ground. As he did so, the dream belt became visible — the belt, with the great Jalis diamond winking beside the clasp.

A sigh of envy ran along the line of Gnomes like wind through grass.

"We will have that, too," said the leader. "Take it off and throw it towards me."

"The belt is the reason for my coming here," Adin said. "I must speak with you. The diamond is the talisman of the Jalis. You cannot — "

"Take the belt off, or die where you stand," the leader growled, her breath smoking in the freezing air.

Adin knew he had no choice. He took off the belt and tossed it onto the snowy ground. The Gnome leader stepped forward and snatched it up, her small black eyes alight with greed. She jerked her head and a red-bearded Gnome darted in to pick up the sword and drag it away.

"Take the prisoner to the post," the leader ordered.

"Bind him well. Make him bleed by all means, if he struggles, but do not kill him. The bait must be alive. The green beast will not touch dead meat."

The other Gnomes closed in on Adin and dragged him to a post set in the ground. It took every one of them to hold him, though they were strong, and the points of two arrows were pressed to his throat.

Adin looked up as they began to bind him to the post. High above his head, a great stone was poised dangerously on the tip of an overhanging rock. He understood their plan and felt sick.

The leader stood alone by the stream, gloating over the diamond in her hand.

"Listen to me!" Adin shouted, in mingled fear and anger. "Our land is in great peril! We must help one another!"

The leader glanced at him scornfully. "We need no help from any outsider," she said. "Our mountain is not in peril, because we are here to defend it. What do we care for the rest?"

"You will care when the Shadow Army controls all but your mountaintop!" roared Adin. "Do you really believe the Shadow Lord will let you be, when that time comes? No! He will send Greers and monsters in their thousands — in their tens of thousands. There will be so many that you will not be able to slaughter them all. And then you will be overwhelmed."

There was a short silence. Adin felt a glimmer of hope. He could tell that his words had made the Gnomes around him think.

"Perhaps it would be wise to give the stranger a hearing, after all, Az-Zure," the red-bearded Gnome said gruffly, at last.

"Be silent, Ri-Thon!" snapped the leader. "The stranger is good bait, and that is all. Why else did we agree to let him live this long? There is no other bait to be had, since the vermin Kin have flown away for the winter."

Seeing that the other Gnomes still hesitated, she frowned.

"Tie him, and take your positions up above!" she ordered. "When the green beast comes, and begins to feast on the bait, we will roll down the stone upon them both and our mountain will be our own once more. Make haste! Even now the creature may have heard the bait's cries, and be creeping up on us."

And at that very moment, something huge and green sprang over the frozen stream and seized her in its jaws. She screamed once, horribly, and the Jalis diamond flashed as the dream belt fell from her hand.

The Gnomes around Adin cried out in shock and horror. They dropped the rope with which they had been binding him and seized their bows.

A shower of arrows flew at the green beast. Some found their mark, but did little damage. Most bounced harmlessly off the scaly green hide.

The beast rose up on its hind legs. It lifted its head and growled, shaking Az-Zure's limp body like a rag doll.

Arrows flew uselessly through the air. Adin pushed aside the loose ropes and dived for the belt. He fastened it around his waist and felt the strength of the diamond surge through his arms. He snatched up his bow, fitted an arrow into it, took careful aim, and let the arrow fly.

The green beast howled as the heavy arrowhead sank deep into its throat. Az-Zure's body fell from its open mouth and thudded to the ground.

"Get her away!" bawled Adin to the Gnomes, fitting another arrow to his bow. "Do not waste time shooting. Your arrows are too light to damage this beast. You know it! Leave this to me."

Out of the corner of his eye he saw a darting movement

as the Gnomes ran to do his bidding.

Then the beast was leaping at him, its orange eyes blazing. Adin stood his ground and let his second arrow fly. It found its mark beside the first.

The beast reeled back, gurgling and choking, raking at its throat with its claws. Then, abruptly, it toppled and fell. It kicked and quivered in the snow for one long moment. Then it lay still.

A great cheer rose up from the crowd of watching Gnomes. Adin picked up his sword and walked to them slowly. His legs were trembling, his mouth was dry, but he wished to show no weakness.

The group parted for him, and he saw that, by some miracle, Az-Zure was still alive. Two Gnomes were supporting her, while others plastered her wounds with pads of bright green moss.

"I tried to destroy you," she croaked to Adin. "And yet you stood and fought for me when you could have escaped. I owe you my life. For the Dread Gnomes, this is a debt of honor that can never be repaid."

"It can," Adin said gravely. "And if you will take me to your caverns, and let me speak with you, you will see how."

And so it was. That very night, the great emerald of the Dread Gnomes found its place beside the diamond in Adin's dream belt, and the tribe swore loyalty to his cause.

So out of hatred and terror came goodwill. The Shadow Lord's creature of destruction had served a purpose its master could never have imagined in his wildest dreams.

How that master would have gnashed his teeth, if he had known!

Then the beast was leaping at him . . .

The Bargain of the Mere

RETOLD FROM *THE DELTORA ANNALS*

he third tribe Adin visited in his quest to fill his dream belt was the tribe of the Mere. How he gained the Mere talisman, the great lapis lazuli, for the belt, is a curious story. It is so curious, in fact, that over the centuries some scholars have claimed that it cannot be true.

These scholars have suggested that Adin's ordeal must have been so terrifying that it caused him to imagine the events he later reported. We now know, however, that there is nothing impossible about Adin's tale.

It happened this way . . .

With the diamond and the emerald safe in the belt, and his purse heavy with Gnome gold, Adin traveled south from Dread Mountain to the great town of Rithmere.

He had no trouble on the road. The countryside of the Mere had been devastated by the Shadow Army. The few souls left in the ruined villages were too busy struggling for survival to challenge a lonely stranger. Perhaps they did not even realize that Adin *was* an intruder from another tribe, for by now he looked as weathered, ragged, and long-haired as they did.

When Adin arrived in the town, he saw that it was surrounded by a high stone wall studded with spikes of broken glass and hideously decorated with the decaying heads of Greers.

Teams of workers were hauling more stones to the top of the wall, building it even higher. The great wooden doors stood open, however, and Adin walked through them boldly.

No one challenged him. No one gave him a second glance, and when he had entered the town, he saw why.

Rithmere was filled to bursting with people who had fled before the Enemy hordes.

Families were living on the narrow streets, their pathetic bundles of possessions heaped around them. Groups of haggard men and women sprawled in doorways, playing games of chance. Children ran wild among the market stalls and scavenged for food in the gutters. Everywhere, starving beggars held up pleading hands.

Adin felt sick at heart as he threaded his way through the milling throngs. Never had he seen such human misery. He listened to every plea for help, and his purse was soon empty. How could he keep riches for himself, while people were starving?

In the distance he heard the roar of many voices. He pushed his way towards the sound and saw that a noisy crowd was gathered outside a large, square building in the town center.

The people in the crowd were jeering and shaking their fists. They seemed to be trying to climb the steps of the building, but were being held back by a line of enormous guards in leather armor.

At the top of the steps stood a fat man, a thin man, and a tall woman. All three were wearing long dark blue robes that glittered with silver specks, like the night sky. Swirls of blue paint decorated their faces and the backs of their hands, their oiled hair fell in ringlets to their shoulders, and heavy silver chains hung about their necks. Despite their finery, they looked angry and fearful.

"Go back to your work!" the woman shouted to the crowd in a high-pitched voice. "We, your elected leaders, know what must be done. The raising of the wall must continue. More weapons must be made. Rithmere must be made safe against another attack. That is our task now."

"No, Zillah!" bellowed a hulking man whose long, wild hair was tied with strips of leather that jingled with good luck charms. "Defense is not enough! For centuries the vermin of the Plains have envied our lands. Now they are sheltering the Shadow Army, and plotting with the Enemy against us! We must attack them — wipe them out, for good and all!"

The crowd burst out in a chorus of high, warbling cries, like the howls of frenzied wolves. Aghast, Adin began to edge around the mass of bodies, trying to get closer to the steps.

"The Plains vermin deserve death!" the huge man shouted. "They are in league with the monsters who tried to destroy us, who killed our families and burned our homes and farms. Yet here stand our cowardly leaders, urging us to huddle tamely in our city instead of taking our revenge!"

"Karol is right!" the woman beside him shrieked. "Dorkin, Loosely, and Zillah are traitors to the Mere! They must be cast down! They must be replaced by new leaders who are worthy of our trust!"

The howls rose in pitch, and the people pressed forward. The leather-clad guards struggled to hold their line. The three leaders glanced nervously at one another and took a step back.

The woman, Zillah, clutched at a large silver star that hung on the chain around her neck, as if seeking protection. Then, suddenly, her eyes fixed on Adin, moving cautiously at the edge of the crowd.

Her face changed, and she pointed eagerly.

"Wait!" she cried shrilly. "See there! That man with the bow upon his shoulder! He is no citizen of the Mere! He is a Plains spy! Take hold of him! Bring him here!"

Immediately, the crowd's attention turned to Adin. He was seized roughly, and in moments he was being dragged up the steps and thrown down in front of the three leaders.

The two men could hardly conceal their delight. The woman kissed the silver star. Adin knew that they were blessing their good fortune. He was just what they needed — a new victim to interest the crowd and make it forget its anger against them.

"I am no spy!" he shouted, staggering to his feet. "And I am not of the Plains. I am Adin, a man of Del. I have come to you with a message — a message you must hear!"

"Indeed?" said Zillah, with a thin smile. "Then tell us your message, man of the south. We long to hear it."

The crowd roared with laughter. Adin knew that he would have one chance to convince them, and one chance only. He raised his head and began to speak.

He told them of his dream. He told them that while the seven tribes of the Land of Dragons remained at war with one another, they could never defeat the Shadow Lord. He showed them the gleaming steel belt. He asked the people of the Mere to allow their talisman to take its place beside the diamond and the emerald.

He spoke as well as he could, but when he had finished he could see he had convinced no one.

The leaders smiled. The huge man, Karol, sneered. The crowd jeered and spat.

Then Zillah whispered something to her companions. They both grinned broadly and nodded. She faced the crowd and lifted the silver star, so that all could see it.

"We should let fortune decide this matter," she

shouted. "That is the Mere way, is it not?"

The people stopped shouting. Their faces grew interested. They pressed forward, listening intently.

Zillah turned to Adin. "Here is our bargain, man of Del," she said, loudly enough for everyone to hear. "We will give you our talisman if you can prove your worth by performing a heroic task. If fate truly intends the belt to be completed, you will succeed. If you are a madman, or have been lying to us, you will fail."

"What is the task?" asked Adin, his heart sinking to his boots.

"Oh, it is very simple," Zillah said with a cruel smile. "You must go to the Shifting Sands and bring back the head of a Sand Beast."

The watching people roared with laughter, slapping their knees and nudging one another.

Adin hesitated. He knew the woman was using him for her own purposes, to amuse the crowd and so save herself and her companions. He had not the faintest idea what a Sand Beast was, but clearly it was something monstrous.

Yet he had no choice but to accept her offer. He knew that if he refused, he faced instant death.

"I will do as you ask," he said, and his spirits sank further as the crowd's merriment increased.

"Excellent!" said Zillah. "Oh, I have no doubt you will succeed! What a fine sight it will be, indeed! We will declare a holiday in Rithmere, I think, so that everyone can enjoy it."

The crowd screamed with savage delight, and in moments they were sweeping Adin and their three leaders out of the town.

They walked for what seemed to Adin a very long time. And then at last they reached a high barrier of huge rocks that stretched away to left and right as far as the eye could see. The people grew quieter, muttering with nervous excitement, and finally falling silent. But still they followed as Adin and the leaders climbed the rocks.

"Here is the place where you are to prove yourself," said Zillah as they reached the top. "How do you like it?"

Adin's mouth went dry as he stared out at the desert of vast red dunes spread before him. A low, droning sound was humming in his ears. A feeling of terror seized him, and his legs began to tremble.

He put his hands on the diamond, for strength, and as he did so he glanced down and saw that the brilliant green of the emerald had faded to murky gray.

He knew what this meant, for the Dread Gnomes had told him that the emerald paled in the presence of evil. He wondered if the place itself was evil, or if the evil was in the minds of the people who had brought him here.

"Go down and try your luck, then, man of Del," jeered the thin, hollow-cheeked leader whose name, Adin had learned, was Dorkin.

"I will need my weapons," Adin said in a low voice.

"We will throw them down after you," said the leader called Loosely, whose round face was gleaming with sweat beneath the blue paint. "Why, how can you behead a Sand Beast without your sword?"

Clearly, this was some sort of joke, for the people around him tittered. But the laughter died away very quickly as Adin clambered down the rocks, and by the time he stood upon the red sand it had stopped completely.

His bow and his sword landed beside him. He retrieved them quickly and looked up. The people of Rithmere were ranged along the top of the wall, their faces alive with cruel excitement.

"Which way should I go to find a Sand Beast?" Adin called to Zillah.

"Any way you choose," she called back. "Soon enough, a Sand Beast will find you."

The people around her grinned and whispered.

Adin turned away from them. Gripping his sword tightly, he moved to the first dune and began to climb it. His feet sank deeply into the soft red sand. Red flies swarmed about him, stinging his face and hands. The strange, droning sound filled his ears.

He fought to keep his mind clear, to pay close attention to everything around him. He remembered the words of Greel the Jalis, repeated over and over during their lessons in swordplay: *Be always on your guard. A warrior's eyes must be everywhere. Small signs may signal great danger.*

He glanced quickly upward. The clear, pale blue sky seemed to shimmer above his head. He looked down again, scanning the red sand to his left and right.

And as he did, he saw, from the corner of his eye, a tiny flicker of movement above him. He froze and looked carefully at the place.

There was nothing there — nothing but a tiny trickle of sand running down the side of the dune, about two-thirds of the way up. It was as if something beneath the dune had moved very, very slightly, disturbing the sand just enough to cause that small, slow trickle . . .

Small signs may signal great danger.

Without thought, obeying an instinct so powerful it could not be denied, Adin flung himself to one side. And in the same instant, the dune burst open in a spray of scarlet sand.

A huge, terrifying creature sprang out of hiding. Sand poured from the joints of its spiny legs. Dozens of eyes like shining mirrors glared in its tiny head.

Its pincers snapped at the ground just where Adin had been standing a moment before. Finding no prey where prey had been expected, the beast made no sound. But its head turned slowly, and its mirrored eyes met Adin's.

In that instant, Adin understood that there had never

A huge, terrifying creature sprang out of hiding.

been any chance for him — not a chance in the world. He had been encouraged to hope only so that his shock and terror would be the greater, when at last he saw the truth.

The Sand Beast was monstrous. It was a thing of terror. No weapon could dent the rock-hard shell that enclosed it. No sword, however skillfully wielded, could sweep that wicked, many-eyed head from its armored body.

Behind him, the warbling howls of the Mere people rose and swelled. This was what the people of Rithmere had come to see — the dreamer of Del, his pride cast down, running in terror from the beast, showing himself to be a fool and a coward.

They will be disappointed in that, at least, Adin told himself grimly, standing his ground and gripping his sword even more tightly. *If I must die, I will die fighting.*

The Sand Beast rose on its back legs, rose to its full, enormous height. It towered above Adin, outlined against the sky. Dozens of swollen, leathery bags swung from the front of its body. Its pincers clawed the air.

Then . . . the sky behind its head seemed to move. Adin blinked, unable to understand what was happening, half thinking that terror had disturbed his mind and his sight. And he cried out in shock as suddenly, with a sound like a clap of thunder, something swooped out of the heavens and snatched the beast from the ground.

The wind of mighty wingbeats threw Adin off his feet and sent him rolling to the bottom of the dune. Sand flew upward in a scarlet cloud, blinding him. He heard a hideous squeaking, tearing sound, and a heavy thump.

The wind died. For a moment there was utter silence. Then there was another sound — the sound of delicate crunching.

Adin staggered to his feet. Sand was falling around him like rain, falling quickly as if it was being sucked back to the ground. He blinked in terror at the vast, glittering shape before him.

It was a dragon. It was not golden, like the dragons of Del, but midnight blue, spangled with points of light, like the night sky. It was feeding peacefully on the Sand Beast, crunching on a spiny leg with relish.

It saw Adin watching it and licked a spine from its lips. "Good day, small man," it said lazily. "What good fortune that you happened to be here today! You tempted my snack out of hiding very nicely, and saved me a tedious wait on high."

Adin could not speak. He could only stare, in mingled awe and dread.

The dragon gave a small, amused snort and began chewing the spiny leg once more. Slowly, Adin began to back away from it. His foot knocked against something. He looked down and jumped.

The head of the Sand Beast was lying half buried in the sand, its mirrored eyes glazed in death. Red flies had already begun swarming around it, and lizards were gnawing at the ragged neck.

A wild idea came to Adin. "Do you not eat the beast's head, dragon?" he blurted out.

"Never," the dragon said with its mouth full. "Some of my tribe do, I know, but all those eyes are not to my taste. I prefer the legs — so deliciously crunchy!"

Adin wet his lips. "Then — may I have the head myself?" he asked.

"Oh, certainly," replied the dragon with a careless flick of one enormous talon. "Will you eat it here, or take it away?"

"I will take it, if you please," said Adin.

"That is good," the dragon said. "I confess, I prefer to eat alone."

It went back to its meal. Adin shook the head free

of lizards and slowly, laboriously, dragged it back across the red sand to the barrier of rocks where the people of Rithmere crouched in terror.

The people watched in awe as Adin hauled the head up the rocks, little by little. No one made a move to help him or stirred a finger. But when at last he reached the top, the three leaders crawled shakily to their feet.

With his foot, Adin rolled the Sand Beast's head to the hem of Zillah's robe. She jerked back, clutching the silver star at the end of its chain. Beneath the swirls of blue paint, her face was bleached to the color of ash.

"I have performed the task you set me," Adin said quietly, and waited.

Still Zillah clutched the silver star and did not speak.

The people began to murmur. Then the huge man, Karol, stood up. He bowed low to Adin, then turned to Zillah.

"Against all odds, the man of Del has performed the task," he said harshly. "Fortune has favored him and proved him worthy. Our fate now lies with him. Give him the talisman."

So Zillah opened the silver star she wore about her neck and took from inside it the Mere talisman — the lapis lazuli, the heavenly stone, the gem of good fortune that glittered like the midnight sky, like the wings of the dragon on the Sands. And she held it out to Adin with a trembling hand.

Adin took the gem and placed it in the belt, beside the emerald. And the savage people of the Mere stared in silence and in wonder, for all could see that it shone more brightly there.

And from that moment on, the Mere was Adin's to command.

The Archer of Azzure

RETOLD FROM *THE DELTORA ANNALS*

One stormy winter's night, the guards keeping watch on the Del city walls saw a rider on a white horse approaching swiftly from the blackness of the west. A cloak billowed about the rider like wings, glittering like ten thousand stars when the lightning flashed and the thunder roared. But above the cloak there was nothing to be seen at all. It was as if the rider had no head upon his shoulders.

The guards' blood ran cold. In all their minds was the thought that the Lord of Shadows had come. But they held their posts, for the safety of Del was in their charge, and they knew their duty.

As the rider drew nearer, the guards began to breathe more easily, for they saw that he was a human man whose head was covered by a black leather helmet that had blended with the darkness.

The helmet dipped low over the stranger's brow and nose, masking the top half of his face. Dark braids of hair ringed with silver bands hung down beneath it. Watchful eyes gleamed behind its eye slit.

When the guards challenged him, the rider slowed his horse, but did not pause. He raised one gloved hand in silent greeting and continued riding to the gates.

The head guard on watch that night was a tall, red-haired young man named Walter. By chance, this was Walter's first time as chief of the watch, and he was determined to show that he was worthy.

"What is your business here?" he shouted to the rider at the gates. His voice was a little more shrill than usual, for he was troubled by the stranger's appearance and his confident manner.

"I beg entrance to the city," the rider said. "I have traveled far and must speak to the people of Del this night. Pray open the gates, and let me in."

Walter was very much surprised, but he reminded himself who and what he was, then straightened his shoulders.

"The people are in their beds as so they should be, so late and on a night like this," he said grandly. "We do not open the gates at this hour. Return in the morning, and we will see."

Lightning cracked the sky. There was a mighty crash of thunder. The heavens opened, and freezing rain poured down. The guards bent their heads and hunched their shoulders, but neither the stranger nor his horse so much as quivered.

"I cannot return, in the morning or at any other time," the stranger said curtly. "What I have to say must be said tonight. It concerns the army which now camps on the Plains, preparing to attack the south as soon as winter gives way to spring. Three other tribes of the Land of Dragons have listened to my words. Will you be the one to deny your tribe the same chance?"

Walter felt sweat bead his brow, despite the freezing rain. What was he to do? He cursed the fate that had brought the stranger to the city gates on just this night.

"You had better let him in, sir," muttered his grizzled second in command, who was peering over the wall beside him. "He is plainly a grand lord from across the sea. If we turn him away, Del might be the only tribe to lose the chance of news that will help defeat the Shadow Army. What will the leaders of the city say to that? What will the people do when they hear of it?"

Walter hesitated for a moment, and then he nodded, and gave the signal for the bars to be taken down from the gates. He did not dare risk denying the people of Del the chance to hear the wise words of this noble stranger.

"Very well," he called. "You may enter. What is your name?"

"You may call me the Archer of Azzure," the rider said, urging his horse through the opening gates. And only then did Walter notice the great bow slung over his shoulder, and the quiver of arrows at his back.

The rider had dismounted by the time Walter had hurried down from the wall to greet him. He looked no less impressive standing on his own feet than he had done while on his horse. In many ways he looked more so.

He was no taller than Walter, but his body, shrouded in the starry cloak, gave the impression of great strength. The braids of hair hung almost to his shoulders. His mouth was firm, with lines in the corners that could have been the marks of laughter or of suffering. The dark eyes gleaming eerily behind the mask of the helmet were the eyes of a man who had stared death in the face.

Tongue-tied, Walter stared at him, suddenly feeling very young.

"Escort me to the meeting hall, if you please," the Archer said as the lightning flashed and the thunder cracked. "Then ring the bells to rouse the people. There is no time to lose."

And his manner had such authority that Walter obeyed without question.

In a very few minutes the bells were sounding in the

market square. Frightened, confused people hurried from their houses, pulling coats and cloaks over their night-clothes, carrying their sleepy children.

The Archer of Azzure stood on the raised platform at the front of the hall, waiting silently as the meeting hall filled. Torches flamed on either side of him. The glass case that held the tribe's talisman rose behind him. Water dripped from his garments disregarded and lay steaming on the floor. His helmet gleamed in the flickering light, and his cloak glittered.

He looked like a figure of legend — a figure of dream or nightmare.

The six members of the city council were scattered throughout the hall. The Archer had taken their usual place, and none of them cared to join him there. Even Master Gabb, the busiest and most pompous of them all, preferred to stay below.

Gabb knew that he did not look his best, with his striped nightshirt flapping wet around his ankles and long strands of hair trailing uncombed over the bald patch on his head. He did not wish to meet the great visitor while he was in this state.

Jealously, he wondered which of the other councillors had called this sudden meeting, and why he had not been informed of it in good time.

As it happened, all the other councillors were wondering the same thing. But, not wishing to seem foolish, or less important than their fellows, none of them asked the question aloud. As the ordinary folk around them murmured excitedly, glancing at them with questioning eyes, they all stroked their beards or folded their arms, nodding thoughtfully and pretending to a knowledge they did not have.

Only Walter and his guards knew the truth of the matter. But they had been forced to return to duty on the

He looked like a figure of legend . . .

wall, for the city could not be left undefended even on a great occasion.

When the hall was full, and the doors had been closed against the pounding rain, the Archer of Azzure began to speak. His words were every bit as thrilling — and as wondrous — as the people had been expecting.

The Archer told of a dream and a magic belt. With a black-gloved hand he drew his starry robe aside and the people gasped as three huge gems flashed in medallions of steel.

There was a diamond, an emerald, and a stone that shone like the night sky. Their beauty was breathtaking, and their power could be felt by every soul who saw them.

The Archer said that these gems were the talismans of the Jalis, the Dread Gnomes, and the Mere. He gestured to the glass case behind him. He asked that the people of Del allow their talisman, the great topaz, symbol of faith, to join the belt, so that the Land of Dragons might be saved from the tyranny of the Shadow Lord.

The people gazed up at him, filled with awe. At that moment there was not one of them who would not have followed him to the ends of the earth, if he had asked them to do it.

The councillors who were nearest to the front of the hall hurried forward and climbed onto the platform. Bowing low to the Archer of Azzure, they walked proudly to the glass case and opened it between them. Then there was a short delay as they argued in whispers about who should have the honor of removing the great topaz and presenting it.

Marooned in the middle of the crowd, Master Gabb stood dripping and steaming, frantically trying to think of something to say or do. He was as enraptured by the mysterious stranger as everyone else, but his injured vanity pricked him.

He had no chance of pushing his way to the front of the hall and joining the people on the platform without making a fool of himself. But he wanted to play some part in the startling events of this night. He did not want the people to know that he had been left out of the decision to welcome the Archer of Azzure.

A question occurred to him at last. He smoothed his straggling hair and cleared his throat loudly, waking a child who had been sleeping on her father's shoulder beside him.

"Could you explain, honored sir, why you have come to Del only now?" he asked, his face growing very red. "Del is the greatest tribe in the land. Surely, we should have been the first to add our talisman to the belt?"

The Archer looked down from his great height, and his lips curved into a wry smile. "I would have preferred Del to be the first," the Archer said pleasantly. "But there were reasons why that could not be."

Gabb bowed, as if perfectly satisfied with the answer, and looked smugly around at his neighbors.

"Why is Master Gabb's face so red, Dadda?" asked the newly woken child, her eyes very wide.

"Hush, Violet," her father murmured as the people around them smothered laughter, and Gabb's face grew even redder.

"But he is *very* red, Dadda!" whispered Violet. "Even his baldy head!"

"Hold your tongue, child!" Gabb hissed viciously. "Be still, or the fierce Archer of Azzure will be angry and eat you up!" He pointed at the dark and silent stranger on the platform.

Violet giggled. "*That's* not the Archingov Enzoo!" she exclaimed. "That's Adin the blacksmith! He would not eat me! He is Dadda's friend. He eats honey cakes from our shop, and makes me a rabbit from his handkerchief, and mends our cart when it breaks."

Shock gripped the room. The councillors by the glass case froze. The Archer of Azzure stood motionless.

"Why did you go away, Adin?" the child called to him, in her high, piping voice. "I was so glad when I woke up and heard your voice, and knew you had come back. But you are wearing very funny clothes, Adin. I liked your old ones better."

People began to blink, as if a spell had been broken. They began to whisper, one to another. They stared at the silent figure on the platform, and this time they ignored the starry cloak, the shining belt, and the helmet of strong black leather.

They looked at the bow slung over the Archer's shoulder and the quiver on his back. They studied the Archer's size and his shape, and the color of his braided hair. They remembered the sound of his voice . . . and then they knew what the child had known long before them.

This was no mysterious stranger. This was no great lord from across the sea. This was an ordinary man of Del. This was Adin the blacksmith!

A great, angry murmur arose in the meeting hall. The councillors on the platform shut the glass case with a crash. Master Gabb, his eyes nearly starting from his head, began to push roughly forward. The other councillors who were still among the crowd were doing likewise.

In moments they were all crowding onto the platform, ready to seize the impostor, ready to tear the helmet from his head and make him pay for daring to trick them.

But the Archer of Azzure held up his left hand, and put his right upon his sword.

"Stop!" he ordered. "Come closer at your peril!"

The councillors stopped, gaping like fish out of water. Gabb was the first to find his voice.

"Do you dare to threaten us, blacksmith?" he spluttered. "Have you taken leave of your senses? Why, I saw through your ridiculous disguise the moment I saw you! I was simply waiting for the perfect moment to expose you."

"Indeed, Master Gabb?" said the Archer calmly. "You hid your knowledge well."

"Liar!" spat Gabb, his scarlet face swollen with rage. "Cheat! Ruffian! Upstart! Dolt! Common, ignorant, dirty-faced blacksmith!"

The Archer nodded. He pulled the helmet from his head and faced the crowd.

"And with those words, people of Del," he said, "Master Gabb has told you why I chose to come to you as a stranger."

The people fell silent. They stared at the familiar face of their blacksmith. It was leaner, browner, and somehow older than they remembered, and the eyes seemed darker and more thoughtful. More than a few wondered what those eyes had seen to make them appear that way.

"Nothing I have told you tonight is a lie," Adin said soberly. "My dream was real. Our danger is real. My quest is real. The belt is real. The talismans of the Jalis, the Dread Gnomes, and the Mere are real, as all of you can see and feel."

He smiled slightly. "Even the name I gave you was a true one, for before I left the Dread Gnomes their leader honored me by naming me the Archer of Azzure, in gratitude because I had saved her life."

He lifted the black helmet in his hand. "This was made for me by the people of the Mere. My cloak was also a Mere gift. I wore them to this place and came to you by night, because I knew that you were far more likely to listen to a mysterious stranger than to one of your own."

He glanced at the panting Gabb. "Especially one of

your own who is only a common, ignorant, dirty-faced blacksmith," he added.

The people moved restlessly. The other councillors frowned and edged a little away from Gabb.

"I had planned to secure your trust — and the topaz — and depart before my real identity was known," Adin went on. "But now, thanks to the keen ears of my good friend Violet, my little ruse has been exposed."

He shrugged. "Perhaps it is best, after all, that this is so. Perhaps I was wrong to doubt you. Only you can tell me that."

He waited. The councillors glanced at one another, but none of them said a word. Then Violet's father spoke suddenly from the crowd.

"I am Samuel of Del, baker, husband of Bella and father of Violet," he said, identifying himself in the way that was customary at public meetings for all except the city councillors. "Like my friend Adin the blacksmith, I am only a common man. But common men can have more common sense than a hundred noblemen put together. And common sense tells me that if we believed Adin's words before, when we knew him not, we should believe them even more now that we know him very well."

The crowd murmured, turning to look at Samuel, turning back to look at Adin.

"I am Nelly of Del, fish seller, daughter of Lisse and Jacob," shrilled a slim, sharp-faced young woman from the back of the room. "We know Adin the blacksmith to be an honest man, a man of sense with nothing foolish or fanciful about him. The Mere and the Gnomes and the savage Jalis did not have this knowledge, and yet they gave him their talismans for the belt of his dream. I believe we should do the same."

Many people were nodding now. The murmuring was growing louder.

"You are mad, all of you!" exploded Gabb, who had been listening with furious disbelief. "This man Adin is our *blacksmith*! Why should he have been chosen to save the land? The very idea is . . . is absurd!"

"Why?" shouted a stout woman, quite forgetting to give her name and title. "Because he is a workingman? Because he is not a soft-bellied, baldy-headed, smooth-tongued councillor? Well, if my fate is to be in the hands of anyone, I would prefer Adin the blacksmith to you any day, *Master* Gabb!"

And this time the people of Del showed their agreement with a roar that shook the timbers of the roof and quite drowned out the sound of the pelting rain.

There was much more talk that night — and much more argument. The storm had blown itself out and the sun had risen before the meeting ended. But at last the will of the people prevailed, and the great topaz became the fourth talisman to join the dream belt of Adin.

Master Gabb fought the decision to the last. When his advice was ignored, he uttered dire warnings of disaster and withdrew to his fine house to sulk.

Later, however, he was to become one of Adin's greatest supporters. As an old man, indeed, he was in the habit of claiming that he had always known the blacksmith's worth, and had been one of his closest advisers from the beginning. And many were the rambling tales he told to his grandchildren, and to those long-suffering souls who shared his favorite tavern, about his great friend Adin, the Archer of Azzure.

The Place of the Spirits

RETOLD FROM *THE DELTORA ANNALS*

aving gained the talismans of the Jalis, the Dread Gnomes, the Mere, and Del for the belt of his dream, Adin judged that his next goal should be the Plains.

The guards and councillors of Del earnestly advised him against this plan. They told him what he already knew — that the Shadow Army was camped in Plains territory, waiting for spring. They told him what he secretly feared — that the Plains would surely mean his death.

But Adin knew that if his dream was to be fulfilled, the talisman of every tribe must become part of the dream belt. The gem of the Plains was needed as much as any other. And surely he had the best chance of securing it while the invaders were resting — and unsuspecting.

By all reports, the people of the Plains had abandoned their countryside to the Enemy. Before winter took hold, some had fled south, into the territories of Del and the Jalis. These poor souls had either been killed or had gone into hiding for fear of their lives. But from the fragments of news they had left behind them, it was clear that the great Plains city of Hira still stood and was well defended.

Hira, then, was where Adin intended to go.

So one cold and sullen morning he set out from the

gates of Del, riding the great white horse that had been the gift of the Mere. His friend Samuel and five members of the city council rode with him as far as the Plains border. But he would not let them come farther. He knew that he must make the rest of the journey alone.

He rode on through scattered patches of snow, seeing no living things but roving herds of the strange beasts called muddlets, until he reached the great waterway called the River Broad.

And there he was forced to stop, for the river was true to its name. It was so wide, and the water was so cold, that he knew he could not swim across. He knew also that his brave horse would sink long before it had reached the far bank.

He could see the shape of a city on the other side of the river. He could see towers and turrets rising behind a cold gray wall. He knew that the city must be Hira.

He could see no sign of Enemy troops surrounding it or swarming on the plain to its north. The Greers, it seemed, had either retreated or had not reached the city before winter closed in to stop their advance.

Adin felt a wave of relief. The situation was better than he had dared to hope. The only dangers he would have to face in Hira were the people of the Plains themselves.

Those dangers would be very real, if the stories of the neighboring Mere tribe were to be believed. But shining in the steel belt Adin wore about his waist were the diamond for strength, the emerald to signal danger, the lapis lazuli to bring good fortune, and the topaz to clear and sharpen the mind. Besides, he had already braved the strongholds of four other tribes and lived. Why should it not be the same with Hira?

If only he could reach it.

But he could not reach it. The cold, swift-running river barred his way, bending in a great curve to enclose the city and the plain on which it stood, on three sides.

Adin followed the river north for a time, hoping to find a bridge or a boat to help him make the crossing. But he found nothing.

The day ended. The sky clouded and darkened, and a huge orange moon rose. Lights twinkled from the city, which now was well behind him. The river changed from gray to black. And still Adin found no place to cross it.

At last he climbed down from his tired horse, removed its saddle and bridle, and saw that it had food and water.

As it ate and rested, Adin tried to do the same. Then he put his hand upon the great topaz, remembering that the gem's power was strongest when the moon was full. The topaz warmed beneath his fingers, but no easy answer to his problem came to him.

He gazed longingly across the river again. A light mist had begun stealing over the water. And suddenly, through the mist, Adin saw a tiny, flickering light.

The light was moving — growing brighter. A boat was coming towards him from the other side of the river.

Slowly, the boat grew nearer, until at last Adin could see the lantern swinging from a holder on its bow and make out the figures of an old man and an old woman at the oars. He waited in suspense as the boat reached the riverbank. The old people turned around to look at him, with eyes that seemed as old as time.

"I wish to cross the river," Adin said.

"Of course," the old woman mumbled. "Why else did you summon us?"

Adin did not explain that she was mistaken, and that no summons had been sent. It was good enough for him that the boat had come.

Quickly, he shouldered his bow and his pack. He whispered to his horse to wait for him if it could. Then he moved to climb into the boat.

A boat was coming towards him from the other side of the river.

"Wait, my fine fellow!" said the old man. "What will you pay us for our work in rowing you across this river?"

"Two gold coins," said Adin, for this seemed a generous price to him.

"Not enough!" the old man said, and spat into the cold gray water.

"Three gold coins, then," said Adin. "I can afford no more."

The old woman grinned a gap-toothed grin. "Around your waist you wear a treasure beyond price, good sir," she said in a sly, wheedling way. "Lend that treasure to us, to hold just for one minute, and we will row you across the river and back twenty times over."

Quickly, Adin covered the belt with his coat. "Row me across the river or not, as you choose," he said roughly. "This treasure is not mine to lend."

The man and woman both bared yellow teeth and held Adin's gaze for a long moment. Then, at last, they glanced at one another and shrugged.

"It is hard that we cannot have our hearts' desire, after waiting for so long," the man grumbled. "But so be it."

He turned to Adin. "Get in," he ordered. "Let this journey be done, so we can rest at last."

Wondering very much, and not a little afraid, Adin climbed into the frail craft. It set off across the water. The thickening mist swirled about it, cold and clammy and smothering all sound but the lapping of the water. The two old people bent to the oars in perfect time.

"Have you lived in Hira long?" asked Adin at last, to break the fearful silence.

"We never lived in Hira," the old woman said, without lifting her head one moment from the oars. "Hira is a wicked place that steals the young and foolish. We bide by the river. But not for much longer."

Adin did not know what to make of this forbidding speech, so he said nothing more.

At last the boat reached the far bank, scraping on the mud. The lantern went out, as if by some signal. The old man and the old woman clambered out of the boat with many weary groans.

Adin hastened to follow them. He found himself knee-deep in long, damp grass. He could see the shadows of bare, knobbly trees nearby, and the dark shape of a house. But the mist was thick, the moon was shrouded in cloud, and he could see no more.

It was bitterly cold. The two old people had disappeared so completely that it seemed the mist had swallowed them up. Adin called to them softly, but received no reply.

Straining his eyes to the left, he thought he could see the faint glimmer of the city lights in the distance. But he could not be certain. Deciding that he would have to wait the night through before attempting to go on, he began to make his way towards the house. No welcoming light shone from its windows, and the idea of asking the two strange old people for a bed was distasteful to him, but he had no choice.

As he moved farther away from the river, he began to feel hard snow beneath his boots. Mist hung all about him like a thick white shroud. The harsh chill made his breath catch in his throat.

He reached the dark house and knocked upon the door. The door swung open under his hand. He moved forward cautiously, calling a greeting, and the moment he crossed the threshold, the room beyond the door began to glow with light.

Adin blinked in amazement. Before him was a tidy sitting room. A colorful braided rug lay upon the floor. A fire crackled in the fireplace, and candles burned on the mantelshelf. Another candle flickered on a table set at the foot of a steep, narrow staircase that led, perhaps, to the attic.

Two worn chairs were drawn up before the fire, and in the chairs sat the two old people who had rowed the boat.

Adin reasoned that they must have been sitting in the dark, hoping he would miss the house in the mist and go his way without troubling them farther. Then, on hearing him enter, they had jumped up to light the candles so as not to appear foolish. The only thing that puzzled him was how they had been able to return to their chairs so quickly.

Later, he was to realize that he had understood nothing at all. And he was to shudder at the memory of how calmly he had stepped farther into that house.

The old people turned to look at him. Their faces were as pale as the mist.

"Close the door," the old woman said sharply. "We are cold enough."

And indeed it was cold in the room — cold as death, despite the candles and the crackling fire.

"I am sorry to intrude," said Adin. "But I would be glad of a bed for the night, if you are willing."

"Our will is of no account," the man said, turning back to the fire and holding out his hands to the blaze. "We must give you what you ask. Take the candle at the bottom of the stair. Your bed is ready, up above."

"It has been ready this long while," murmured the woman. "May you sleep well in it. And then may we sleep, too, at last."

She, too, turned back to the fire and held out her hands to the flames, as if hungry for warmth.

Realizing that his hosts planned to say no more, Adin murmured his thanks, picked up the candle, and climbed the steep stairs.

At the top of the stairs was a small attic bedroom with a low, sloping ceiling and a narrow iron bed. A cracked mirror hung on the wall above a wooden shelf. Mist crawled behind the tiny, barred window.

It was a grim little chamber in its way, but it was warmer than the room downstairs, and to Adin it seemed strangely welcoming.

He closed the door behind him. Finding it had no lock, he put his heavy pack against it, so he would hear if anyone tried to enter. Then he pulled off his boots, put out the candle, and lay down upon the bed, with his sword near to hand.

He had intended merely to rest, for he did not trust the strange old people whose eyes had dwelled so eagerly on the jeweled belt. But his day had been long, and at last, just before dawn, he slept.

And he dreamed.

He dreamed of rainbow gems scattered on a wooden floor. He dreamed of a veiled face looking out at him from a cracked mirror. He saw gray men swarming in their thousands from the shadows beyond the mountains. He saw a pack of Ak-Baba attack a rainbow dragon above the broad river. He saw Hira lying in ruins, and a great evil dwelling within its walls. He saw the Lord of Shadows, red eyes burning with hatred.

He saw salvation — strong arms beating white-hot steel, and seven spaces in the steel, waiting to be filled.

He woke in terror, sweat soaking his clothes and hair. Light was shining onto his face. At first, in his confusion, he thought he had left the candle burning. Then he realized that the light was sunlight shining on him from above . . . through a ruined roof, open to the sky.

Gasping, he looked around him.

He was lying on a mass of rags and rotten boards. A cracked, blackened mirror hung on the wall. The remains of rusted bars jutted from the windowsill like crooked teeth. The door against which his pack had rested was hanging from its hinges, eaten to paper thinness by white worms.

Gripped with horror, Adin scrambled up, thrust his feet into his boots, gathered his belongings, and ran from the room. The steep staircase crumbled to dust beneath his feet. He fell heavily, tumbling onto freezing earth and stones.

He looked around him. He saw the shell of a room, a collapsed roof. He saw the stones of a fireplace and chimney, thrusting towards the pale, cold sky.

Stunned, hardly knowing what he did, he crawled from the ruined shell and looked towards the long, gray river. He saw snow, earth, long grass, and a cluster of bare, knobbly trees whose branches clattered together in the wind. On the riverbank he saw a clutter of ancient wood that might once have been a boat. And on the other side of the water he saw a small white shape — the shape of a horse with a bent head, quietly cropping the grass.

And hardly had he begun to face what all this meant when he heard two things. He heard a low buzzing, coming from somewhere beyond the trees. And he heard human voices, approaching from the direction of the city across the plain.

He took his sword in his hand and stood upright. He knew that this was what he had to do, though his knees were trembling and his head was spinning.

Around the ruined house came a group of men and women. All of them wore wigs of smooth gold threads. All of them wore long, stiff, embroidered robes and costly jewelry. All of them had their arms crossed over their chests, their hands hidden inside their robes' wide sleeves.

All of them looked afraid.

When they saw Adin they stopped. Their eyes widened. Their faces grew pale and blank.

The one who had been leading took a breath. "Are you a living man?" she asked in a low voice.

Adin nodded. "I am Adin of Del," he managed to say calmly.

Three of the woman's companions withdrew their hands from their sleeves. They were all holding long, curved knives.

The woman, however, did not take her eyes from Adin.

"How did you come here, man of Del?" she asked, still in that same low voice.

Adin knew that it would be wisest to speak the exact truth, though he did not know what these people might make of it. He did not know what to make of it himself.

"I came from the other side," he said, pointing over the water to his horse. "Two old people rowed me across the water in the dark."

"And here you spent the night?" asked the woman. She sounded breathless.

"Indeed," said Adin. "The old people gave me a room. They seemed to feel compelled to do it, though I do not know why. And now I find that . . . that it was not a room at all, but part of a ruin. It did not seem that way last night. I do not pretend to understand it."

"In Hira, we saw the lights, glimmering across the plain," the woman said, still in that same breathless voice. "This is a place of dread to us. It is called the Place of the Spirits. It was cursed long ago, and it's the haunt of killer bees and the ghosts of the dead. Even the Greers recoil from it, and it has so far kept them back from the Hira plain. There have not been lights here in living memory. But there were lights last night."

She glanced at her companions. "We thought, perhaps,

that the Greers had at last found a way to defy — "

She broke off. Her eyes widened in horror as she stared at something behind Adin.

Adin swung around. The sky before him was black — black with bees. The bees were sweeping towards him in a thick mass, and through the branches of the trees more were flying, and more.

The low humming he had heard before had become a dull roar.

His eyes widened with fear. He raised his hands to protect his face, to try to beat off the fury of the swarm.

They know you. They will not harm you. Be still.

The voice sang softly in his mind. And with the voice came a picture — a veiled girl, looking from a mirror.

And suddenly, Adin knew who she was. He knew what this place was, too. And he knew why the two old people had been condemned to wait for him, to row him across the river, and to do for him whatever he asked. He remembered the second power of the topaz — the power to call forth the spirit world. He understood and was filled with awe.

Humbly, he lowered his arms, and he waited.

The swarm reached him. It hovered before him, making shapes in the air. But not one bee landed on his body. Not until he bent his head. And then, reverently, in threes and fours, bees settled on his arms, his chest, his back, and his shoulders till his clothes were thick with them.

He could feel the creatures' warmth flow through him. He could feel their energy and their will. His ears were filled with the sound of the rest of the swarm flying about his head.

Slowly, he turned to the people of the Plains. Their faces were frozen with astonished fear.

"Who are you?" a man breathed.

"I am a descendant of a woman named Opal who lived here, in this place, long ago," Adin said. "Opal dreamed of a time of terror that now has come to be. Her parents tried to silence her and were doomed to linger here until the day that I should come, bearing the land's salvation."

He showed the belt beneath his coat as bees swarmed around him like a living shield. The people of the Plains drew sharp breaths of wonder as they stared at the four gleaming gems in their medallions of steel.

"The people of ancient Hira would not listen to Opal the Dreamer when she came to them warning of the approaching terror and telling them what they must do to save the land," Adin said. "Now I have come to you in my turn. Will you listen to me?"

"We will," the woman said. And her companions agreed, like whispering echoes.

So Adin returned with them to Hira, that doomed, walled city that was then still in its prime.

The people of the city saw their leaders escorting him and the bees flying about him like a guard. In their hundreds they followed him to the great hall. Shopkeepers, builders, menders, makers, cooks, jewelers, children of every age — all crowded after Adin in awestruck silence. Even the city's rat catcher left his grim and lonely work to see the wonder.

Adin walked into the great hall with four gems shining in his belt. He walked out, just an hour later, with five. The rainbow gem of the Plains, the symbol of hope, had taken its place beside the topaz of Del, completing a circle that had begun long, long ago.

The bees left him then, for they had done their part. They flew back to the Place of the Spirits.

They were its only guardians now. The troubled shades who had wandered its ruins and its ancient trees had done their part also — and were at peace at last.

The Ralad Wilds

RETOLD FROM *THE DELTORA ANNALS*

din the blacksmith did not know what to expect when he journeyed from the Plains into the territory of the Ralad people. In those days, in the Land of Dragons, little was known of the Ralad tribe, or of its huge territory.

The haughty people of the Plains spoke of their neighbors with disdain. They said that the Ralads were an ignorant, backward people, small and thin, blue-gray in color, ugly as goblins, and very poorly dressed.

They said that if Ralads met strangers in their land they did not stand and fight, but simply melted away into the trees. They said that the Ralads appeared to have no weapons, and had made no effort to build roads through their territory, or to protect themselves from invasion. Their domain was as wild and overgrown as if no one lived in it at all.

Finding that Adin was still determined to seek the Ralad talisman for his dream belt, the Plains leaders escorted him back across Broad River. There they caught muddlets for themselves to ride, by tempting the three-legged beasts with apples. Very grateful that he did not need to do the same, Adin saddled and mounted his waiting horse.

They rode together to the Ralad border. There, the snow-covered fields of the Plains gave way to tangled forest that rang with birdsong despite the winter chill.

"And this is only the beginning of the wilderness," said Fie, the most outspoken of the Plains leaders. "It is a shocking waste. The Ralads have no ability to use their land as it should be used. And they are too timid and ignorant to defend it. Many a time we have been tempted to take some of it for ourselves."

"But you have not," said Adin. He meant it as a compliment, but the Plains leaders seemed to take it as a criticism, for all of them frowned.

Fie smoothed her golden wig with a careful hand. "We abandoned attempts to settle the Ralad Wilds long ago," she said stiffly. "Plains explorers of the past suffered all manner of ill fortune — broken bones, near drownings, injuries in thickets of thorns, starvation when they lost their way, and so on. Not to mention that the territory is infested by scarlet dragons, which range the skies unchecked."

"It is a treacherous, miserable place," agreed one of the men. "The Ralads are welcome to it."

Adin nodded thoughtfully. He had begun to wonder whether the Ralads were quite as ignorant as the people of the Plains supposed.

Beneath the first trees of the forest, at the beginning of a narrow path, he made his farewells.

"There is still time to turn back," said Fie impulsively. "Forget the Ralads. Return with us to Hira, I beg you. The Ralad Wilds are treacherous, and surely thick with Greers."

"Indeed," said one of her companions. "You will not find what you seek here, Adin of Del. Even we of the Plains, with all our weapons, soldiers, and other defenses, lost many thousands when the Shadow Army invaded.

It would be a miracle if the Ralads were not wiped out entirely. Any who fled their town before the Army reached it would soon die of cold and hunger. Mark my words, if a Ralad talisman ever existed, it is surely in the hands of the Enemy by now."

Adin's heart lurched at that, but he let nothing of what he felt show on his face. It was important that the Plains people did not lose their faith in him, or fear for the precious gem they had given into his keeping. And there were other reasons for him to show nothing but confidence.

"The belt must carry the talismans of all the seven tribes if the Shadow Lord is to be defeated," he said firmly. "So I saw in my dream, and so I am sure it will be. I do not believe the Ralads would have let their gem fall into Enemy hands. I think they are far too clever for that."

"Clever!" jeered Fie.

"More clever than you know," said Adin.

And with that, he raised his hand and left them, urging his great horse slowly along the narrow, winding path until they were out of sight. Then he swung down from the saddle, took a long stick from the ground, and began to walk, leading his horse after him.

He walked slowly, tapping the ground before him with the stick, like a blind man finding his way. And many times over that day his patience was rewarded as the point of the stick detected holes, traps, snares, and false turnings in his path.

It was as he had thought. The Ralads were far from defenseless. They used the land to help them repel invaders. Their false paths led enemies into swamps and over cliffs. Their traps tipped invaders into holes and pools, and tripped them into thornbushes and great drifts of snow.

For centuries this clever means of defense had protected Ralad lands from the people of the Plains. But soon Adin began to fear that it had not been enough to protect them from the Shadow Army.

The farther into the forest he went, the louder the caroling of the birds seemed to grow. But the chorus of shrill whistles and low, fluting songs was not enough to mask another sound — the low, growling sound of hundreds of voices, not very far away.

It is better to know the worst than to remain in ignorance, Adin told himself. And slowly, though the path seemed to be trying to turn his feet another way, he pushed towards the sound.

After a time, his horse became unwilling to follow him. It snorted, tossed its head, and dug its hooves into the ground.

"Come, Wing," Adin crooned.

But the great white horse would not go forward. And so at last Adin was forced to leave it, telling it to wait while he trudged on alone.

He began to smell smoke. Then he saw ahead of him a snowy bank, which seemed to overlook a large clearing in the forest. Smoke was drifting upward from the clearing, and the sound of a great, muttering crowd was now very loud.

Adin crept forward, keeping low. He lay on his belly and crawled to the top of the bank.

In the last rays of the dying sun, he saw what was below. And sickness rose in him as he realized that he had found the town of the Ralads — or what remained of it.

He could see that once the little town had been a beautiful place — a wonder of small, rounded houses and halls built along neat, paved streets. Every building had been made of curved mud bricks that fitted so perfectly together that the joins were almost invisible. In the middle of the central square was a shallow pool that must have reflected the sky like a mirror, not so long ago.

Now the pool was fouled with ash, bones, bricks, and broken pottery. The houses were in ruins, with smashed windows, splintered doors, and burned-out roofs. Small heaps of broken furniture burned along the streets and in the square. And pressed together around the blazing fires were hundreds of huge, pale soldiers wearing helmets and breastplates of dull gray metal.

Adin knew they were Greers. He had never seen a Greer before, but no one could mistake those grunting sounds, those shapeless faces, those hairless bodies that looked as if they had been roughly fashioned out of clay.

It was just as the people of the Plains had predicted. The Ralad defenses had failed. The town had been overrun, and the Ralads had either been killed, or had fled into the forest, to perish in the cold.

Shivering and heartsick, Adin stared down at the ruined village.

The Greers were sullenly gnawing at lumps of some sort of food. Most were half naked, shivering in the freezing air. A few of the luckier ones had filthy blankets draped around their enormous shoulders.

The blankets were small and had once been brightly colored and patterned. No doubt the Greers had dragged them out of the ruined houses, just as they had taken the tables, stools, beds, and benches that now fed the flames of their fires.

Adin jumped as a high, cracked voice spoke from somewhere very near.

"It will snow again tonight, and they are burning all that remains of the dry wood," the voice said. "The brainless fools! More of them will freeze tonight — and even more tomorrow."

"Let them die," another voice growled. "They are

doing nothing here but eating, sleeping, and squabbling in any case. And the stink of them makes me sick. The master will send fresh troops as soon as this cursed winter ends."

The voices were coming from just below where Adin was lying. Cautiously, he eased his body forward and peered down.

There stood a man and a woman, both closely wrapped in cloaks lined with some sort of fur. The woman wore a patch over one eye, and her teeth were black and jagged. The man's face was red and pinched with cold. His fair mustache and pigtail were stiff with frost.

They are human, Adin thought, a terrible anger rising within him. *Yet they have bowed their knees to the Shadow Lord. They led his vile hordes to this town, and they watched as it, and everyone in it, was destroyed. They are the worst of traitors.*

His gloved fingers gripped the snow. A desire he knew to be madness seized him. He wanted to draw his sword — to leap down upon the two traitors and kill them where they stood.

A piercing birdcall sounded behind him, cutting through the growling sound of the Greers, and recalling him to his senses. He steadied his breathing and deliberately relaxed his hands.

"I cannot think why we were ordered to stay in this wilderness, Wrass," the woman said in a low, complaining voice. "Why can we not go back to the main camp, to wait with the rest of the Army?"

"It is the master's will that we remain," the man called Wrass said shortly.

"But there is no sense in it!" the woman exclaimed. "The village is destroyed. No Ralads who returned here would find shelter now. And you and I know very well that none will return, in any case. They are all dead of hunger and cold long ago. When they fled they took nothing with them — not even the blankets from their beds. Why, some had not waited to put on their boots!"

Her companion chuckled. "We took them too much by surprise," he said with a touch of pride. "It was a fine plan to attack by night."

"Perhaps," muttered the woman fretfully. "But they escaped us in the dark, and there were no bodies for the Ak-Baba to see in the morning. If there had been, the master might not have insisted we stay."

She looked at the Greers with loathing. "If only we had proper troops, instead of these disgusting objects," she hissed. "If only they were faster, and could move more quietly. If only their eyes were not so weak, and all but useless in the dark."

"They are strong," her companion said. "They know how to fight."

The woman spat. "And that is all they know," she said. "There is not one of them who has as much brain as a brute beast. The master was too impatient. He should have perfected them before invading. Then we would have destroyed everything in our path, and reached the south coast long before this endless winter began."

Her companion frowned. "Take care, Sheela," he muttered. "It is dangerous to voice treacherous thoughts. Even here, we are not out of the master's reach." Nervously, he glanced at the sky.

The woman bit her lip and shivered.

Adin lay still. The fire of his anger had died. Now all that remained were the bitter ashes of despair. Dimly, he wondered if he could move back without alerting the two leaders to his presence. It was a risk, but he knew he had to take it if he wished to live. Already his body was growing numb with cold.

"Sheela!" the man hissed suddenly.

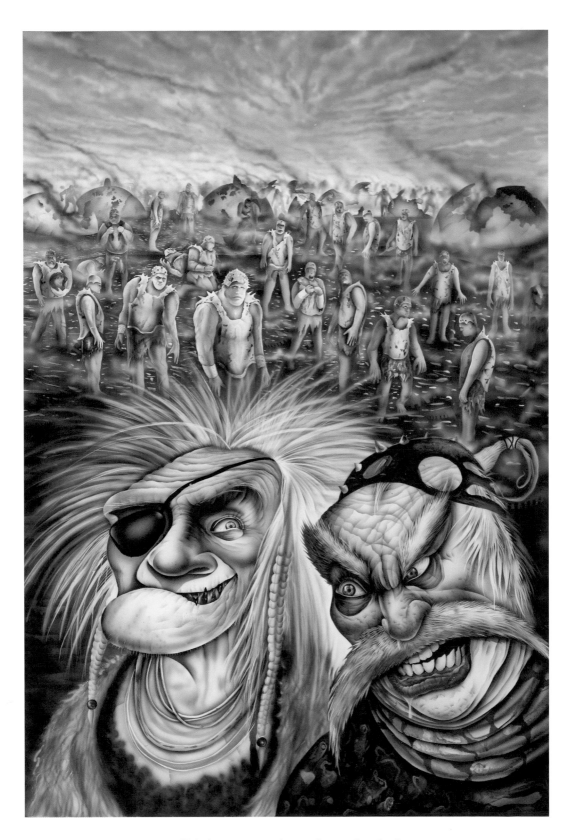

"It is dangerous to voice treacherous thoughts."

The woman looked up and gave a whimpering cry. Adin looked up also. His skin prickled. A dark, terrifying shape was silhouetted against the brownish-gray of the snow clouds. It was circling the village. Adin saw a lashing tail and huge, beating wings.

"Ak-Baba!" The woman's face was twisted with horror.

Wrass cursed. "You fool, Sheela!" he said furiously. "Why did you not hold your traitorous tongue? Now you are finished!" Abruptly, he turned and began floundering away through the snow.

"Wrass, no!" the woman shrieked. "Stay with me! Help me to explain!"

She stumbled after the man, catching at his sleeve, but he tore himself free and pushed her away from him with such violence that she fell to the ground. She squirmed in the muddy snow, screaming piercingly. The Greers turned their heavy heads to look at her curiously.

"Master, I am not disloyal!" the woman shrieked, covering her head with her arms. "I did not mean what I said, I swear it!"

The man, Wrass, was still struggling away from her, putting as much distance between them as he could.

Adin knew that this was his chance. He forced his numb body to move. He wriggled down the bank and crawled painfully back the way he had come.

Snow had begun to fall. Sheela's wails still pierced the air. Every moment Adin expected to hear her scream as she was snatched up by the Ak-Baba's talons and borne away to her doom.

But that sound never came. Sheela's wailing went on and on. Then Wrass's voice rose in a bellow of surprise.

"Wait!" he roared. "It is not an Ak-Baba! It is a dragon! A scarlet dragon! Sheela, get up! Troops, arm yourselves!"

The Greers began to howl. Steel clattered and rang as they seized their weapons.

Adin staggered up. His feet felt like cold stones, but he began to run, stumbling as fast as he could to the place where he had left his horse.

When he reached it, Wing was gone.

Adin blinked, unable to believe his eyes, unable to accept the disaster that had befallen him. He had planned to mount his horse and ride with all his might back to the land of the Plains — to turn his back on failure, and leave this wild territory of despair with all speed.

Now he would have to make his way on foot, in falling snow, at the mercy of the brutal cold that even now was pinching his face and turning his limbs to ice. Unless . . . unless he could track Wing down. Surely, the horse had not strayed far.

He did not dare to call, or even to light a torch, but in the dimness he could see hoofprints leading off into the darkness.

The snow was falling faster now. He knew that if he did not make haste, the prints would be covered. His eyes on the ground, he began to hurry along the horse's trail. And he had taken no more than three or four steps when some sort of heavy cloth fell over him from above, covering him to his knees.

He shouted and flailed in shock. But it was no use. In moments ropes were binding the cloth fast about his chest, his waist, his thighs, tying up the top half of his body like a package.

He cursed the panic that had made him such easy prey. Why had he not guessed that guards would have been set around the Greer camp? How could he have been so careless?

The ropes pulled at him. He felt hands pushing his back, his legs. His captors wanted him to walk.

Swiftly, he considered falling to the ground and refusing to move. But that, he feared, would only make death come more quickly. No doubt he was being kept alive only so that he could be presented to the leaders for questioning.

So he shuffled through the snow, blind and hobbled, desperately trying to form a plan of escape. Through the muffling cloth he could hear the howls of the Greers in the camp and the calls of night birds. But his captors were utterly silent.

It seemed to him that the agonizing walk went on forever, though surely he was only a few minutes away from the ruined village. His mind spinning in confusion, he felt himself moving upward. His ears were filled with a strange, roaring sound. Then he gasped and staggered as needles of icy water rained over his head and shoulders.

Hands steadied him, and he was pushed downhill.

Then, suddenly, everything stilled. He heard a strange, soft whispering. Then the ropes that bound him loosened and fell away. The damp, suffocating cloth that had covered him like a shroud was lifted up and cast aside.

"Welcome," a voice said politely. "Pray forgive the rough handling you have received. We do not care for our whereabouts to be known."

Adin blinked. For a split second, he thought that he had flown back in time. He was standing in the midst of a paved square, beside a mirrorlike pool. All around him were rounded houses, so cleverly made that it was almost impossible to see the joins between the curved bricks.

And facing him was a large number of small, blue-gray people, with orange-red hair and earnest, coal-black eyes. They seemed to be waiting for him to speak.

Adin swallowed. He remembered all he had thought, before this nightmare began. He forced his clumsy, confused mind to work, and at last he saw how things were.

"You are . . . the Ralads," he managed to say at last.

The small people nodded, waiting.

"This is your true town," Adin said. "The other — the one the Greers have taken — was a copy. You never lived in it. You built it only to deceive them."

The faces around him broke into smiles.

"That is so!" exclaimed a young woman. "Long ago, we saw spying Ak-Baba fly over our town. We heard Plains people on the border speak of invasions in the north. We knew that one day the Enemy would come to us."

"Yes!" an eager young man chimed in. "So we prepared. We built another town just like our own, for the Enemy's army to find. We built it as far away from our real town as was needed to ensure our safety, but near enough to deceive the Ak-Baba."

"It is a miracle," Adin murmured. "It is . . . incredible! To build a whole town . . . as a lure! To build it so perfectly that the Enemy never suspected . . . "

"It was the work of many years," a wizened old man said modestly. "But it was necessary. The Ralads are not fighters. We have always defended ourselves by other means."

"We built beneath a shelter, in secret," a woman added. "And when the false town was finished, complete with furniture, and pots and blankets, and garments, and bread for the tables, we unveiled it, and at the same moment we hid our true town from sight."

She looked up. And Adin looked up with her and saw a net threaded with leaves stretching overhead, making a barrier between the village and the sky. Snow lay thickly on the net now, but even when the snow melted, the town would be invisible from above.

He shook his head in wonder.

"So you see, Adin of Del," the woman went on, peering up at him slyly. "You were right. We truly *are* more clever than the Plains people know."

Her companions laughed at their visitor's startled expression.

"You were listening, at the border!" he exclaimed. "You heard me talking to the people of the Plains. You knew where and who I was, from the very beginning!"

"Of course," said the old man, his black button eyes twinkling merrily. "You seemed harmless enough, and plainly the Plains people trusted you. But harmless-seeming folk make the best spies, and the people of the Plains are easily deceived. We thought it best to watch and wait a while before greeting you. We have learned to be wary."

"Then we saw your anger as you looked down at the Greers' camp," the young woman said softly. "And we knew that your heart was good. We feared you would be captured. So we called a dragon to assist us, to distract the Greers so you could creep away from the camp unnoticed."

She gestured with the flute in her hand. Adin remembered all the birdcalls he had heard in the forest, and realized that they had not been birdcalls at all, but messages sent from one Ralad to another. At the same time, he grappled with the knowledge that these strange, small people spoke of calling dragons as easily as others would speak of calling a horse or a dog.

The thought reminded him of Wing. "My . . . my horse," he said. "Is he safe?"

"The beautiful four-legged beast is called 'horse,' is it?" said the old man as the other Ralads murmured with interest. "That is good to know. He is quite safe, Adin of Del. He is enjoying shelter, warmth, and food at present."

"Do not be troubled because he left you," the young woman said anxiously. "He was unwilling at first, but we explained that it was for the best, and so he came."

Adin swallowed. His head was spinning. "There is

much I do not know of you," he said at last. "You are a mystery to your neighbors."

"As they are a mystery to us, in many ways," the old man said peacefully. "They fight the land to make it serve them. We cannot see why they do this, when the land provides so freely, if it is treated with respect."

He smiled. "But enough of that," he went on. "You are wet, and no doubt hungry, too — as hungry as 'horse' was, I have no doubt!" He looked around at his friends as he pronounced the new word, and beamed as they nodded in appreciation.

"We will make you comfortable," he went on, rubbing his hands. "And then we will add our talisman to the belt of power."

The calmness with which these words were spoken startled Adin as much as anything else that had happened. He stared around at the watching Ralads, not knowing what to say.

"We know that our safety here cannot last forever," a tiny, plump woman said, seeing his bewilderment. "If the Enemy is not stopped, our village will at last be discovered, and we will be lost. For a long time we have known in our hearts that our only hope was to unite with others to try to repel the invader. We just did not know how to begin."

She put her head on one side. "We have been thinking, however, that perhaps you are our beginning, Adin of Del. You and the belt, whose magic we all felt the moment we laid hands on you. We will give you our talisman, but be warned. We can pledge no weapons, no gold, and no warriors to the cause. We have none of those things. We can pledge only ourselves."

Adin looked into her small, wise eyes. "That will be a pledge beyond price," he said.

And he meant it with all his heart.

The Magic City

RETOLD FROM *THE DELTORA ANNALS*

his is the true story of what happened when Adin the black-smith at last gained entry to the magic city of Tora, seeking the Toran talisman for his dream belt.

The tale is known to few. Though Adin recorded it in *The Deltora Annals*, the ancient Torans wanted it to be forgotten, and historians and teachers have bowed to their wishes ever since.

But, as we have learned, it is unwise to forget any part of our history, however uncomfortable it may be. The truth, and the whole truth, must be told and remembered if we are to avoid repeating the mistakes of the past.

The Torans of the present understand this only too well and bitterly regret that this tale was kept from them in their youth. Because it was no part of their education, they could not benefit from its lessons when their own time of decision came.

The story goes this way . . .

Adin had entered Toran territory early in his quest, only to be driven out by Toran magic. At that time, he carried only the Jalis diamond in his dream belt.

By the time he crossed the Toran border for the second time, however, his belt held five more talismans — the

. . . as he drew closer to the vast, gleaming marble walls of Tora . . .

gems of power that had been the land's gifts to the Dread Gnomes, the Mere, Del, the Plains, and the Ralads.

Only the gem of Tora was missing. And Adin knew that he had little time to secure it, if his dream of rescue for the land of dragons was to be fulfilled.

The unnaturally long winter was ending at last. It was as if the land had tried its best to aid him, but could no longer delay the melting of the snow.

Soon the Shadow Army would be on the move once more. New troops of Greers would stream across the mountains to add to its numbers. The Ak-Baba would return. The terrible might of the Shadow Lord would cast its darkness over the land.

Adin knew that the dream belt had to be complete before this happened. He had to force the Torans to listen to him. There was no time to waste.

As he urged Wing, his great white horse, towards the magic city, he waited for the pain of a Toran banishing spell to pierce his mind. He braced himself for the battle of wills that he knew must come.

But no pain came. Instead, as he drew closer to the vast, gleaming marble walls of Tora, he felt a strange tug in his mind, as if someone — or something — was calling him on.

Wondering very much, he dismounted and led Wing into the broad, echoing tunnel that formed the city's only entrance.

No guard challenged him. No gate barred his way. But Adin felt a cold, eerie tingling run through his body from his boots to the top of his head, and realized that the city was well protected, nonetheless.

He emerged from the tunnel blinking and shaken. He felt Wing nudging at his shoulder, as if the great horse, too, was dazed by what had just happened.

The glory of Tora lay before him, bathed in light — a

vision of broad white streets, marble buildings, sparkling fountains, and masses of delicate flowers.

Out of the shimmering light moved a group of tall, slender people. Their long, flowing robes were richly colored. Their hair hung down their backs like veils of black, gray, and white. Their dark eyes regarded Adin with calm interest.

Adin bowed, fighting down his nervousness. "Greetings, people of Tora," he said. "I am Adin of Del. I thank you for allowing me to enter your city."

The people turned and walked to a vine-hung courtyard, beckoning him to follow.

A fountain played in the center of the courtyard, and flowers spilled from marble urns set in each corner. On one side of the fountain was a bench drawn up to a table on which stood a platter of fruit, a jug, and a cup. On the other side lay a basket of oats and a trough of water for Wing.

Plainly, Adin thought, *we have been expected.*

The people gestured to Adin to sit at the table. He did so, but they remained standing. He looked at them carefully.

At the front of the group was a middle-aged woman in green, a man in scarlet, and a blue-robed older woman whose hair was shining white. Behind were two younger men and a young woman.

Adin caught his breath. The young woman wore a purple robe. Her hair was like black silk. Her eyes sparkled beneath slanting brows, and there was a determined aspect to her mouth. She returned his startled, admiring gaze. Her lips softened as if she would have liked to smile.

The woman in the green robe cleared her throat to claim Adin's attention.

"I am Lenore of Tora," she said. "And I speak for us

all. The fortune-telling stones told us you would come to our land again, man of Del."

Adin tried to collect his thoughts. "The first time I came, you drove me away," he said, being careful not to sound as if he resented it.

"Indeed," the woman agreed calmly. "And we would have done so a second time. But as you entered our territory we felt a yearning to draw you closer. Why this might be, we do not know. Perhaps you can explain? By speaking to us, you speak to all in Tora. Our minds are linked."

Adin's heart leaped. He had always believed that the magic people of Tora would understand at once the mystery of the dream belt. Now he was certain that the seventh talisman would soon join the others.

"The answer is here," he said.

He pulled aside his coat to show the six gleaming gems in their medallions of steel. Eagerly, he told of his dream and his quest.

As he spoke, the expressions of the Torans did not change. No one said a word. Slowly, Adin began to feel uncomfortable, but he forced himself to go on.

"The snows are melting," he finished at last. "Soon the Shadow Army will continue its progress south. If we do not act quickly, the land will be overwhelmed by the evil that dwells across the mountains."

"No evil can enter Tora," Lenore said, half smiling.

"Perhaps not," said Adin. "But everywhere else — "

"Tora provides for all our needs," the woman broke in smoothly. "We have no interest in anything outside it."

There was a general murmur of agreement.

Lenore held out her hand to the fruit and the jug. "Please refresh yourself before you depart, man of Del," she said.

It was a clear signal that the meeting was over. Adin could hardly believe what had happened. The Torans had heard what he had to say and had rejected it totally. They were not going to add their talisman to the belt, and they did not intend to discuss the matter further.

Strangely, he did not feel angry. He did not feel anything but a mild sadness. Yet how could that be, when all he had struggled for was about to come to nothing?

It is this place, he thought suddenly. *It is this city. No evil passions can exist here. All is peace and perfection.*

And yet . . . and yet he could still feel that tug in his mind that he had noticed while he was far from the city walls. It was weaker now, but it was there.

"Someone in the city is not satisfied with your decision," he said suddenly. "I feel it."

"You are mistaken," Lenore answered, and this time there was a touch of coldness in her voice. "We are all of one mind."

"He feels the yearning of the amethyst," said a clear voice.

It was the young woman at the back who had spoken. The two young men beside her stirred uneasily. The silver-haired woman frowned. The man in red froze. But Lenore appeared unmoved.

"That is understood, Zara," Lenore murmured. "There was no need to repeat it. Our decision has been made. The discussion is over."

"But if the amethyst still yearns for the other gems our visitor wears in his belt, should we not think again?" the young woman answered, raising her chin with a touch of defiance.

"The decision has been made, my daughter," the man in red said, recovering himself and speaking with quiet authority. "The great amethyst feels the presence of the other gems and is attracted to them. This does not mean it is right that it should join them. The amethyst belongs in Tora. It is our talisman."

Adin saw his chance. "Surely it is the talisman of all your territory," he said quickly. "Toran land extends far beyond this city. You claim ownership, and the right to decide who enters it and who does not. Therefore, it is your responsibility and your trust. And outside your marble walls, the countryside is ravaged. People have suffered and died, villages have been burned, and there will be more death still if — "

"Enough!" Lenore held up her hand and Adin felt his throat close. Try as he might, he could not say another word.

"Please leave us now," the man in red said. Then it was as if shutters had closed in Adin's mind. Darkness overwhelmed him. When he came to himself again, he was lying propped against a tree outside the city, with Wing snuffling uneasily beside him.

Wincing, Adin stood up. He felt bruised all over — bruised in his mind, as well as in his body.

He saw that while he had been in Tora, the weather had changed. It was cold and damp. Mist had rolled in from the river. Drifting white clouds now surrounded the city walls and hung low over the lake. The trees were ghostly shapes, and the sky was hidden.

Then he saw something gliding towards him through the mist. At first it was just a wavering shape. Then he realized that it was three people, moving very fast and very close together.

One of them was Zara. The others were the two young men who had been standing with her in the courtyard.

Zara's eyes were wide and startled looking. Her silky hair was damp with mist, and the hem of her purple robe was wet. She was shivering. The two men were also shivering, and both of them kept looking around, as if amazed by what they saw.

Why, I do not believe they have ever left the city in their lives before! Adin thought in wonder. And as the three reached him, Zara's first words showed him that he was right.

"What is this clinging whiteness?" she cried. "And this — this wetness on the ground? Has the Enemy caused this? Is this the devastation you spoke of?"

Adin shook his head. "It is quite natural," he said. "It is only mist."

The three Torans looked at one another, then back at him.

"Mist," Adin repeated. "An uncomfortable accident of the weather — like rain, hail, or snow."

But he could see by the blank looks on the young people's faces that this explanation meant nothing to them. In Tora, it seemed, there was nothing that was uncomfortable — and nothing that was natural, either. The weather above the magic city was kept as pleasant and controlled as the life within it.

Zara swallowed and made an obvious effort to calm herself. "This is my brother, Shim," she said, putting her hand on the arm of the taller of the two men.

"And I am Kayan," the other man said, between chattering teeth. "Zara was determined to speak to you further. She was determined to leave the city. We agreed to accompany her."

The expression on his face showed plainly how much he regretted this decision.

"I was made uneasy by what you said of the people who live outside the city," Zara said. "If they are truly in danger — "

"They are," Adin said firmly. "Nothing is more certain."

Zara's eyes seemed to darken, and two bright spots of color appeared on her cheeks.

"They are not our kin, Zara," Shim said soothingly.

THE RISE OF ADIN

"They are merely the descendants of foreign settlers and shipwrecked sailors who came to our territory without invitation, and were allowed to remain. They are nothing to us."

"Do not say that!" exclaimed Zara furiously. "They are part of the land that is our trust. By hiding ourselves away in the city which has become all things to us, we have blinded ourselves. We have betrayed the gem of truth, which was the land's gift. I see that now, and you should see it, too!"

Ignoring her brother's startled expression, and Kayan's gasp, she turned to Adin.

"What will you do now?" she demanded. "The belt is not complete. You have six gems only."

"Then six will have to be enough," said Adin. Ruefully, he looked down at the belt. The hairs rose on the back of his neck as he saw that the emerald had dulled, and that the great ruby had faded. The gems were warning of evil and danger.

Adin put his hand to his sword and looked quickly around him. If Torans shared their thoughts, the people in the city must be aware that Zara, Shim, and Kayan had left the city. Perhaps they were even now coldly planning to put an end to Adin's interference in their tranquil lives.

He opened his mouth to speak, but suddenly, Zara threw up her hands.

"Evil — above!" she exclaimed.

At the same moment, the light dimmed. Then, with the terrible sound of huge, beating wings, a dark shadow swept over them.

A foul, bitter smell filled the air. The mist that clung to the treetops swirled violently, and the trees themselves began to toss and thrash, showering Adin, Wing, and the three Torans with broken twigs and torn leaves.

"What is it?" Zara cried in terror.

"Ak-Baba!" Adin gasped. He turned to Shim and Kayan who were clinging together, staggering and dumbfounded. "Run!" he shouted, pushing Zara towards them. "Get back into the city! The wind will blow away the mist. Then the beast will see us. It will . . ."

The shadow passed, turned, and came back, circling lower, directly overhead. The beating sound was like the roaring of a storm, and a dire chill surged through the mist, piercing their very bones.

Adin could not stand against it. He fell to the ground. Struggling vainly to draw his sword, he squinted upward, through the rain of falling leaves. Wind beat upon his face. Above, the mist surged and tumbled. But, miraculously, it did not part.

He twisted his head to one side and felt a thrill of shock. Zara, Shim, and Kayan were still standing. They were clinging together, their robes flying around them, snapping in the wind. Their long hair flew wildly about their heads; their faces were drawn and pale. But their eyes, unmoving, were fixed on the clouds above.

They were holding the screen of mist in place. Gripped with wonder, shivering with fear, Adin watched with streaming eyes as they fought the wind. They looked so frail, so slender. But the murderous creature above the clouds could not break their will.

Long minutes of agony passed. But at last the shadow lifted and moved on.

Then all that was left was a disgusting stench, like the smell of burning hair and dust, and the slow drifting of the last fallen leaves.

Zara, Shim, and Kayan fell away from one another and crumpled slowly to the ground. Adin crawled to his feet and ran to them. They were still breathing, but only faintly. In anguish, he fell to his knees beside them and took Zara's cold hand.

"Stand away from her!" a sharp voice said.

Adin looked up. The mist was full of robed figures. Lenore was at their head. Beside her was the man dressed in scarlet — Zara and Shim's father.

Unwillingly, Adin stood, then moved back.

"You tempted my daughter from safety, Adin of Del," the man said coldly as his companions bent to gather up the three limp bodies. "Then you brought evil down upon her, and upon her brother and his friend. I hope you are satisfied."

Adin raised his head. "I would give my life for Zara to be unharmed," he said in a trembling voice. "But I did not ask her to come to me. She came because she did not care for the thought that your city was to become an island of peace in a sea of war and wickedness. She understood what you do not."

"And what might that be?" asked Lenore, raising her eyebrows disdainfully.

"That, try as you might, you cannot separate yourselves from the land you live in," Adin said grimly. "What use is safety when it is a prison? What use is comfort, when it can only exist in ignorance?"

Lenore stared at him. "You insult us like the savage you are, man of Del," she murmured. "We regret that we ever saw your face. Mount your horse and go."

So Adin left the land of the Torans for the second time. He left with rage and grief in his heart, tormented by his failure and by the memory of Zara's pale, unconscious face.

The seventh medallion gaped empty in his belt like a wound. And with every moment that passed, the yearning tug of the great amethyst of Tora weakened in his mind, until at last he could feel it no more.

The Battle for Deltora

RETOLD FROM *THE DELTORA ANNALS*

he great conflict that was to become known as the Battle for Deltora was fought in the heart of the land, on the plain of Hira.

The main winter camp of the Shadow Army was just to the north of this plain. Adin the blacksmith believed that the moment the snows melted, the army would storm southward, without waiting until fresh troops came from the Shadowlands to swell its forces.

When, by chance, he had overheard two servants of the Enemy talking in the Ralad Wilds, he had learned much of value.

One of the things he had learned was this: After centuries of planning in his vile domain, the Enemy had grown impatient. The Greers, the shambling warriors he had created to do his will, were still imperfect. Yet he had launched his great attack, nonetheless, relying on their strength and numbers to gain victory.

And until the freezing winter had stopped their progress, the Greers *had* been victorious. They had over-whelmed the countryside of the north. Only the cities and the largest towns had been able to stand against them.

Adin was certain that the Shadow Lord's impatience for victory had not grown less over the long waiting time

. . . in his vile domain, the Enemy had grown impatient.

of winter. In fact, the Enemy's burning need to triumph had no doubt increased because of the forced delay.

That was one weakness. And there was another weakness, even more important.

The Shadow Lord's early victories had certainly fueled his vanity. Adin was certain that by now the Enemy had become supremely confident that nothing could stand against him. He did not know that a great change had occurred in the Land of Dragons over the long winter.

He did not know that six of the seven warring tribes had united against him. He did not know that, for the first time in history, message birds were flying between the territories. He did not know that people were crossing tribal borders without hindrance.

He did not know that when, driven by his impatience, his army of Greers began its new charge, it would no longer be fighting one tribe at a time, but six tribes together.

The Dread Gnomes might still be suspicious of all people other than themselves. The savage folk of the Mere might still hate their old enemies of the Plains. The haughty members of the Plains tribe might still despise their gentle Ralad neighbors. The Ralads might find the ways of other tribes foolish and hard to understand. The lively, free-thinking people of Del might still believe all other tribes were stiff-necked and ignorant of the wider world. The warrior Jalis might still regard themselves as the only real fighting force in the land.

But all of them respected Adin. All of them had listened to him and seen the truth in what he said. All had agreed to put aside their differences in an effort to drive out their common enemy. All had placed their tribal talismans in Adin's dream belt, and this had become a sign of their common purpose.

The six gems in the belt were linked by chains of steel. The six tribes were linked by their belief in Adin.

Only the people of Tora had chosen to hold themselves apart. Only their talisman, the great amethyst, was missing from the belt.

It was a bitter disappointment to Adin that his dream of uniting the seven tribes had not been fulfilled. It was hard to accept that the army of the Land of Dragons would not be aided by Toran magic, as he had hoped.

But there was no time to waste on regrets. The winter snows were all but gone. He knew that the day of reckoning, the day for which he had been planning so long, was fast approaching.

The Ralads had reported that the Greers who had kept guard in their territory were gone. They had been told to return to the main camp, and had crossed Broad River by North Bridge, the only bridge to span the river in those days.

Adin himself had seen an Ak-Baba patrolling Toran skies, the Dread Gnomes had seen two of the foul birds fly over their mountain, and several more had scanned the Hira plain. Mere and Plains spies had sent news that the great camp was suddenly a hive of activity as stores were packed and weapons made ready.

Plainly, the Shadow Army was stirring, preparing to move. The battle for the Land of Dragons was about to begin.

The tribes' battle plan had been made by the Jalis, improved by Adin, and accepted by all the rest. Every tribe had an important part to play, and the first stage had begun before Adin set out on his last, fruitless journey to Tora.

From Dread Mountain, from the Mere, from Del, and from Jaliad, troops moved towards the Plains.

The troops traveled by night, and they did not march like soldiers. They moved in small, straggling groups and by different roads. Their garments were shabby. Their armor, supplies, and weapons were hidden inside ragged bundles heaped on battered carts.

They looked like helpless wanderers who had been driven from their homes by war. No spying Ak-Baba who happened to see them could guess their real purpose.

By the time Adin himself reached Hira, the first stages of the plan were complete.

The Ralads had destroyed North Bridge the day after their enemies crossed it, thus ensuring that the Shadow Army would have to overwhelm Hira and seize its boats if it wished to cross the River Broad without delay.

Mere fighters and Dread Gnomes were waiting in hiding to the north and west of the Shadow Army camp. Already they were in their thousands, and more arrived to join them with every dawn.

All but the youngest and oldest Ralads had been secretly rowed across Broad River to the Hira plain. They were working by night on the second task Adin had assigned them before he left their village.

The land between Hira and the river bend was littered with rough shelters that looked like the dwellings of homeless folk. In fact they were filled to bursting with Jalis warriors.

And the huge, walled city itself was now crowded not only with Plains people, but with the army of Del. The Ralads were there, too, but they were seldom seen in the streets. They slept by day, and at night slipped out of the city gates like shadows to complete their mighty work.

A few Ralads, and the best fighters from each of the other tribes, gathered in Hira's huge dining hall the night before the Greers were expected to make their move.

Adin sat at the table's head. He was gripped by a strange feeling of unreality as he stood up to propose a toast to the tribes' success.

How strange it was to see wary Dread Gnomes,

savage Jalis warriors, and ferocious people of the Mere at the grand feasting table of the great stone city! How strange to see small, blue-gray Ralads side by side with tall Plains leaders wearing stiff, embroidered robes and golden wigs! How strange to see familiar faces from Del in such a setting!

He had brought them to this place. The Dread Gnomes had left their safe, protected stronghold. The Ralads had done the same. The Jalis and the best fighters of the Mere and of Del had left their own cities almost unprotected to come to the Plains.

They had done so because they believed in Adin. On the morrow, they would all learn whether he had led them to victory — or to disaster.

Not for the first time, the words of Master Gabb, councillor of Del, slid, hissing, into his mind.

This man Adin is our blacksmith! Why should he have been chosen to save the land? The very idea is . . . absurd!

Perhaps it is absurd, Adin thought. *Perhaps Gabb is right after all.*

He became aware that he had been standing silent for far too long. The faces at the feasting table were all turned to him. Everyone was waiting for him to speak.

He knew what they were expecting. They were waiting for him to rouse them to fever pitch. They were waiting for him to say that he knew, knew in his heart, that tomorrow would be a great victory.

He could not say it.

He looked down, fighting for calm. He stared at the belt at his waist, and lowered his free hand to touch the empty medallion beside the clasp. The Toran amethyst, symbol of truth, had been denied him. Was this because he did not deserve it? Because his whole quest had been a mistake? A well-meaning blunder, based on a blacksmith's dream of glory? Based on a lie?

Cold sweat broke out on his brow. He jerked his hand away from the empty medallion and clutched instead the diamond on the other side of the clasp.

Strength flowed through his arm, and spread, filling his body with warmth. The diamond gleamed under his fingers like sunlight sparkling on water. Beside it, the emerald shone green as the forests of the land; the lapis lazuli, the heavenly stone, glowed with stars like the night sky; the topaz was gold as the sun . . .

Adin looked up. "We do not know what tomorrow will bring, my friends," he said, raising his voice just enough for everyone to hear. "But we know that the time of running and hiding from the invader has passed. We know that it is time to stand and fight, not only for the sake of our homes and loved ones, but for the sake of the land itself. And we know that separately we are weak, but together we are strong. These things we know. And that is why we are here."

The room was utterly silent. Adin raised his goblet. "Let us drink a toast," he said.

With a great clattering of chairs, the people rose to their feet. They waited.

"To strength," said Adin. "To honor. To good fortune. To faith. To hope. To happiness. May these blessings shine among us tomorrow, as their symbols shine now in the belt that is the sign of our unity."

And from every throat came a shout so loud that it is said the roar made the rafters of the great room tremble.

Birds came at dawn, with the news that the Shadow Army was on the move. By midmorning, the sound of dull chanting mingled with the thunder of marching feet was rolling over the Hira plain. To the watchers from the city walls, the army looked like a vast shadow, sweeping towards them from the north.

The shadow faltered at the edge of the plain, at the ruined farm called the Place of Spirits. Then it swept on, for it had found nothing to fight and nothing to fear. The ghosts that had once struck terror into the hearts of the Greers and their leaders had gone from that place, and the fierce bees that swarmed there remained among the budding apple trees and did not attack.

The commander of the Shadow Army did not waste time or energy wondering at this good fortune. He looked ahead, across the shimmering plain.

He saw that a long, high hill of earth and stones now stretched across the middle of the plain. Ranged along the top of the hill were orderly rows of Plains warriors.

There might have been a thousand of them — a tenth of the number they faced. Splendid in their silver armor and white-plumed helmets, they waited, the sun glinting on their polished spears, swords, and shields.

The commander laughed aloud. His name was Trell, and he was a fine-looking man. Gold bands were clasped around his wrists, and gold hoops hung from his ears. He rode a tall gray horse, once the pride of a Rithmere chief whose bleached skull now swung from Trell's saddle. His eyes were as cold as stones. His ancestors had been mountain bandits. His only loyalty was to himself.

"There is the rampart the Ak-Baba told of, Sheela," he said to the woman who rode beside him on a chestnut mare. "So, do you believe it now? The fools really are going to try to prevent us reaching the city. The Greers will taste blood sooner than expected."

The woman frowned. "I cannot understand why they have left the safety of Hira," she said. "They succeeded in repelling us before."

"Only because the snow overtook us!" Trell snapped.

"And no doubt they know that this time we will not withdraw. By now they must have realized that they made a huge error in destroying that bridge. Now we need their boats to cross the river. And they raised the master's fury by trying to thwart him. He wants Hira's destruction before anything else."

The woman's eyes were on the unmoving silver lines of the warriors ahead. She was still frowning.

"Fury is not a good reason to attack," she said. "Our move south should have been delayed until the bridge was repaired. Hira is strong, and our forces have been weakened by the winter. Besieging it could waste more time than it gains!"

"It is not your place to judge, Sheela," Trell said coldly.

"But it could be that the bridge was destroyed to force us to come here," the woman argued. "Have you thought of that, Trell? Has the master thought of it? These people are more cunning than you think."

"Perhaps you would care to explain all this to the master personally, Sheela?" hissed Trell, glancing at her with narrowed eyes.

The woman gave him a frightened, resentful look, then fell silent.

Trell turned his face away from her. He reflected that he had been wise to keep Sheela close to him, as Wrass had advised. Her months in the Ralad Wilds, away from the main army camp, had done her no good. Her isolation had made her believe she had a right to think for herself.

He could do nothing about her now. Her Greers were accustomed to her. It was possible that they might turn on him if he struck her down before their eyes.

But after the city was taken . . . then it would be time to do something about Sheela. And her Greers, too, if necessary. There were not so many of them left, after all. The hard winter in the Wilds had seen to that.

He could hear the Greers grunting and snuffling excitedly behind him. He realized that they had stopped chanting and had picked up speed.

Their weak eyes had at last sighted the enemy. They were thirsting for battle. Battle was what they had been bred for. It was all that gave them pleasure.

Trell could hear Sheela and the other human leaders shouting to their troops, ordering them to keep step. He knew that Greers would not obey for much longer.

He ground his teeth in frustration. He would have liked to stay in front of the army to see the way ahead clearly. But that had become too dangerous. He would have to move aside and reach clear ground as quickly as he could. At any moment the Greers would stampede, crushing all before them.

"Trell!" cried Sheela urgently. Already she was turning her horse's head, ready to flee.

He was tempted to order her to stay where she was, then abruptly changed his mind. Sheela was a good fighter. She might as well survive to make herself useful in what would be her final battle.

Together he and Sheela galloped across the front line of Greers till they reached safety.

Just in time. As Trell turned to face the city once more, he heard the sound of rhythmic crashing. He was astounded to see that the sound was coming from the Plains troops. They were beating their shields with their spears, insolently taunting their enemies.

How did they dare? What did they think to gain by maddening the Greers even further? They had made some high ground for themselves, certainly, but they could never defend it against such odds. Steep as that hill was, the Greers would scale it in an instant! This would be a massacre! This would be a sight worth seeing!

Grinning, he shrank back as the Greers howled and

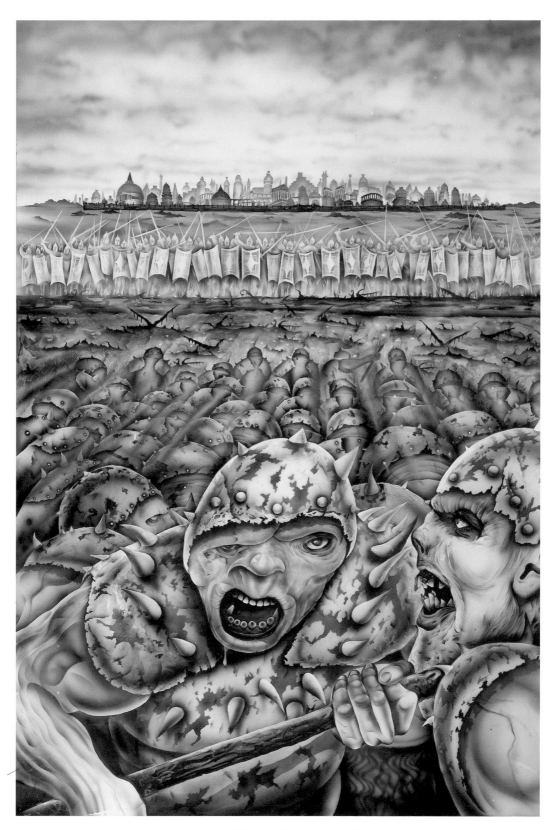

This would be a massacre!

broke ranks. Like a huge pack of ravenous beasts, froth spraying from their gaping jaws, they thundered towards the slim, silver lines of the enemy.

The Plains troops did not stir. They faced the oncoming hordes with their heads held high. And still they beat upon their shields, beat and beat, driving the Greers into a frenzy.

Despite himself, even as he looked forward with relish to their slaughter, Trell admired them. *Had I troops like this, what a commander I could be!* he thought. *These soldiers think, and they feel, and yet still they stand—*

"Trell!" Sheela shouted over the roaring of the Greers rushing past them. "Trell, we must try to stop this! I fear — "

"Be silent!" he roared, enraged. "Your foolishness is as great as your face is ugly! What you think, what you fear, means nothing! You mean nothing! Do you hear?"

Sheela shut her mouth with a snap and said no more.

The gap was closing between the Greers and the defenders of the city. Trell watched greedily, running his tongue over his lips. They were just moments apart. Soon, soon . . .

The Greers at the head of the horde bellowed in triumph. They leaped forward.

And then they disappeared. Hundreds of them simply disappeared!

Trell's eyes bulged in his head. He saw more Greers vanish, and more. And it was only then that he realized what was happening.

A great, long crack, deep and wide, had opened in the earth, just in front of the hill. It must have been covered with some fabric, which had then been scattered with dust. The fabric had collapsed under the Greers' enormous weight.

Sweat broke out on Trell's forehead. Shock and rage battled within him.

"Halt!" he roared. "Fall back!"

But the Greers were too maddened to listen. The troops at the back continued to hurl themselves forward, snarling and spitting, fighting to get to the taunting enemy. By the time they saw their danger, they could no longer avoid it. They fell, screaming, into the pit, shock showing for a brief moment on their brutish faces before they plunged into darkness.

"Trickery!" howled Trell. "Danger! Halt!"

He glanced at Sheela, frozen-faced beside him. "Do something!" he roared. "Stop them!"

"How can I stop them?" the woman said softly. "I mean nothing. You told me so yourself."

Trell urged his horse forward. He reached the edge of the yawning pit and began waving his troops back, bellowing to them to go around the hill, to go around it! But he doubted they could even see him. They had eyes only for their enemies.

Thousands of Greers had been swallowed by the pit. Perhaps a quarter of the army had been lost. The pit was huge — vast!

Why did I not wonder where the earth and stones for the hill came from? Trell thought in horror.

He wiped the sweat from his eyes. His legs felt like jelly. Desperately, he tried to make excuses for himself. The Ak-Baba had reported the hill. But they had not seen it being made, because the work had been done at night. No one had suspected what lay in front of it. By day, the pit had been too cunningly disguised.

And how could anyone have thought that the people of Hira could construct such a trap? Trell would not have believed them capable of it. It was almost as if other, expert hands had helped them. But how could that be?

At that moment, he caught a glimpse of gray flesh inside the gaping hole and gasped in horrified relief. The crack in the earth had shocked him so much that he had almost begun to believe that it was bottomless — a thing of sorcery.

But it was not bottomless. He could see that now. The pit was filling with bodies. The Greers who tumbled into it now were not being killed by the fall. Rather, they were being killed by other Greers falling on top of them and smothering them.

It was a horrible sight, but Trell welcomed it. Soon the pit would be full to the brim. And then . . .

"Forward!" he shouted madly, beckoning as if the stampeding Greers needed encouragement. He shrank back, watching as hundreds more gray bodies fell, and the pit slowly filled.

He looked with loathing at the city across the plain. He could see that the walls were lined with watchers. He shook his fist at them. "You will not escape us!" he bellowed. "Only wait . . . "

As if his voice had been a signal, a bell clanged. The lines of silver-armored soldiers turned smartly, slid down the other side of the hill, and began to run back towards the city.

"Cowards!" Trell roared, beside himself with rage. But some Greers were clambering out of the pit now. Every moment more were trampling over their comrades' senseless bodies and scrambling up and over the hill to chase the fleeing enemy.

Trell shouted in triumph. Wave upon wave of Greers were crossing the filled ditch now. Already the plain on the city side of the hill was thick with them.

He spurred his horse on, skirting the pit and the hill and galloping along beside his army. There had been a delay. There had been losses — grave losses. But Hira was doomed in any case — Hira, the ragged tent city behind it, and, best of all, those insolent, silver-armored warriors. The Plains soldiers were running swiftly, but they would not reach the city in time to save themselves, and they were still vastly outnumbered.

The city gates began to swing open.

"Faster!" Trell roared to the Greers. "Get them before they reach safety! Do not let them escape!"

Then his jaw dropped. The fleeing soldiers had abruptly halted, and turned to face their enemy. And more troops were pouring from the city — thousands more. Some wore the silver armor of the Plains, but many did not. These others were more roughly dressed. They were armed with spears and heavy swords quite unlike the elegant weapons of the silver army.

There are not so many fighters in all the plains, Trell thought wildly as the swollen army moved slowly forward to meet the Greers. *Where have they come from?*

There was a shout from the city walls. Hundreds of figures rose into view — dark, stocky figures with bows and arrows. Arrows whistled through the air, and every arrow found its mark.

The Greers at the head of the pack fell dead. The Greers behind them stumbled over the bodies and crashed to the ground, to be trampled in their turn by the crowd behind. More arrows flew, and more.

Trell cursed and shouted instructions, but he might as well have been cursing the wind. The Greers were too enraged to listen to anything but the roaring of their own blood. Most seemed not to realize that there was any danger from above. Their eyesight was too poor to see it.

Those who escaped the arrows ran, howling, to meet the defenders of the city. The clash of steel and the screams of the wounded rose hideously as battle was joined.

The Greers fought with their usual savagery. But

always before there had been at least ten of them to every one of their foes. They could not understand why this fight was different from every other they had experienced.

And still the arrows flew, and still more Greers died before they reached their goal.

"The archers on the battlements are not Plains folk," said a voice beside Trell.

He whirled around. Sheela was looking up at the city walls, a slight smile on her lips.

"Who else can they be, you fool?" Trell spat. "Hira is a Plains city. The master told us that the tribes cross each other's borders only in peril of their lives. And we have seen this for ourselves!"

"Plains people are not so skilled with the bow," said Sheela, almost dreamily. "Besides, these archers have powerful arms and shoulders, but are far too small in stature to be Plains folk. I think they are Dread Gnomes."

"You are mad!" muttered Trell.

Sheela shrugged. "Surely you have noticed that the fighters who came out of the city were not all from the Plains?" she said. "A few, at least, were of the Mere. Many others were neither Mere nor Plains. And I think the small, blue-colored creatures who are carrying away the wounded are Ralads from the Wilds. It seems that there is something that we, and even the master, did not know."

Trell pointed with a shaking finger at the Greers still pouring past him like a boiling gray wave.

"It does not matter," he hissed. "Those archers can slaughter thousands, and still we will prevail. Our numbers are overwhelming."

Sheela laughed. He gaped at her and saw that she was still looking at Hira. Slowly, he turned his head. His mouth went dry.

Hundreds of huge warriors in golden armor were surging onto the plain from behind the city. They were closing in on the Greer army from both sides, like monstrous, avenging furies.

Despite their size — and the weight of their shining armor — the golden warriors moved with incredible speed. In moments they were carving their way through the flanks of the Shadow Army with terrible, practiced ease, working together like the parts of a well-oiled machine.

"So that is what a Jalis knight looks like," Sheela said with interest. "Well, it seems we have fallen into a trap, Trell. We are surrounded on all sides."

He stared at her. She nodded, almost brightly.

"Enemy troops have closed in from behind," she said. "Many are on horseback. They are Mere fighters, I think, by their wild looks. Some Dread Gnomes are with them, I suspect, for I saw arrows flying before I came to tell you the news."

"It cannot be," Trell whispered.

"It is," said Sheela. "Greers in the rear are falling in their hundreds every moment. And the rest are being stung to madness by bees — black clouds of bees from the Place of the Spirits. It is almost as if the bees were part of the trap!"

She smiled horribly, showing all her black, jagged teeth, then turned her horse's head away.

"Where are you going?" Trell panted. "Stay where you are! I order you to remain!" He turned his sword on her. His head was spinning. There was a roaring in his ears.

"My Greers are all dead," the woman said. "They were among the first to fall into the pit. I am not needed here."

Again her mouth stretched into that awful smile. "You have been outwitted, Trell," she added softly. "I tried to warn you. But then, what I think does not matter, does it?"

With a roar of rage, Trell lunged at her, piercing her to

the heart. The smile did not leave her face. "Thank you," she whispered. "Better this quick death than the fate which awaits you at the master's hands."

She slumped over her horse's neck and slowly slid to the ground. Freed of its hated burden, the chestnut snorted with pleasure and galloped away.

From the walls of Hira, Adin watched the slaughter on the plain. Beside him stood Padge, the old Ralad who had supervised the digging of the great pit in the plain.

"Did you see that, Adin of Del?" gasped Padge. "That leader on the gray horse-beast drove his sword into the woman with the eye patch! He killed her! But she was on his side! Why would he do such a thing?"

"I do not know," said Adin slowly. "Perhaps. . . he is afraid."

"And so he should be!" Az-Zure of the Dread Gnomes strode up to them, grinning fiercely. "We are winning! Your plan has worked to perfection, Archer of Azzure!"

"So far, it has," Adin agreed. But he did not smile.

Az-Zure put her hands on her hips and glared at him. "What troubles you?" she demanded. "Is it that you are forced to watch the battle from above, instead of fighting yourself? Why, we discussed this till we were tired! It was decided that you would be of far more use here, where you could see all that happened, and give commands accordingly. The timing of the different attacks was vital to the plan!"

"I know that," said Adin with a sigh. "I accepted it."

"Then is it the killing?" Az-Zure persisted. "There have been deaths on our side, certainly, but there have been far more on the other. And surely you did not expect that no lives would be lost in this battle? Certainly, the warriors did not expect that. They knew full well the dangers they faced."

"And the Ralads are doing their best for the wounded," Padge put in. "We are carrying them to safety and tending them as best we can."

"I grieve for the dead, but that is not my only concern," Adin muttered. "The truth is, I fear what might be ahead. There is something wrong here. Where are the Ak-Baba? By all reports, they have always accompanied the Shadow Army in the past. Yet there is no sign of them."

"They may come yet," Az-Zure said grimly. "And if they do, my archers will be ready for them, never fear." She jerked her head at the tubs of oil that lined the wall, each tub bristling with rag-wrapped arrows. Then she hurried away.

"Perhaps the Greers will surrender soon," Padge murmured, his eyes on the battle.

"I fear they will never surrender," Adin said. "I do not think they know how to do so. They were created to fight, and they will keep fighting until they no longer have breath in their bodies."

"But their leaders are human," Padge argued. "That man on the gray horse, for example — the one you said was afraid. He was riding at the head. Perhaps he . . . "

Adin shook his head. "Whatever he may wish to do, he will not do it. Even if he could control the Greers, which plainly he cannot, he must answer to his master in the Shadowlands."

"The Shadow Lord is far away," said Padge.

"The Shadow Lord is a powerful sorcerer," said Adin. "The Greers are his creations. He — I cannot help but feel that he must have sensed what is happening here. If he has . . . "

As he spoke he looked again out to the plain. And then he saw a low, gray cloud on the horizon, ringed and pierced with scarlet light. The cloud was touching the ground. It was sweeping towards the city very fast, and seven fearsome shapes wheeled above it.

A chill ran down Adin's spine. He drew a sharp breath. "Az-Zure!" he shouted. "Beware! Ak-Baba!"

He heard the Dread Gnome's answering cry and saw torches flame along the walls. He rang the bell of warning to alert the troops on the ground of coming danger. But as he did, he knew it was too late — too late for the soldiers to withdraw and too late for flight.

The cloud was already rolling across the plain. Adin could smell the stench of the Ak-Baba as they soared above the confusion of the battle. The foot soldiers at the rear — Mere folk, Dread Gnomes, and Greers alike — were turning, screaming, falling to their knees. Horses were rearing and shrieking in terror, their riders desperately trying to calm them. Black swarms of bees were swirling in confusion.

And now he could see shapes within the cloud — gleams of green, and bulky figures in metal helmets and breastplates. He caught his breath at the power of the sorcery that could sweep new and terrible forces into the battle in the twinkling of an eye. Then he felt the presence at the cloud's center, felt the malice streaming from it like cold breath, and it was as if his blood had turned to ice.

Beside him, Padge drew a long, shuddering breath. Az-Zure and her archers seemed frozen where they stood.

The Ak-Baba swooped, snatching and tearing at screaming soldiers on the plain, then soaring back into the air with dripping beaks and talons, screeching in triumph. The cloud lifted from the ground. Thousands of fresh Greers stood blinking in the sunlight for a split second, then sprang into the attack. Seven green-scaled beasts leaped forward with them, snapping their terrible, grinning jaws.

Adin stared, transfixed, clutching the hard stone of the wall. The sight below was so terrible that the images seemed to burn his eyes. But he could not turn away. He could not move at all.

"It is far better that we tried, than that we did not," Padge's voice said quietly beside him. "We made our choice. And there is not one person here who regrets it, Adin. Except you, perhaps."

Stiffly, Adin turned his head. The old Ralad was nodding. His face was sad, but quite peaceful.

"You take too much upon yourself, my friend," he said gently. "This was not your quest alone, but the quest of all of us, together. Were we to allow ourselves and our children to be enslaved? Were we to abandon our land to this?"

He gestured at the boiling cloud, the slavering Greers, the screeching Ak-Baba.

Adin pushed himself away from the wall. He looked down at the belt. The emerald was gray as ash. The ruby was palest pink. But the diamond, the lapis lazuli, the topaz, and the opal flashed in the sunlight, dazzling him.

Blindly, he put his hand on Padge's shoulder. He turned to face the motionless archers.

"Az-Zure!" he roared. "Rouse yourself! This is not over yet!"

Az-Zure started, as if waking from a dream. She ran her hand through her hair, snatched up a flaming torch, and barked an order. The archers stirred, and reached for oil-dipped arrows.

"Padge, stay and watch by the bell," Adin muttered. Briefly, he squeezed the old Ralad's shoulder. And then he turned and ran down from the wall, down to the city gates.

The time had come for him to join his troops. He

could no longer watch from a lofty height. He would fight with them — to the last drop of his blood.

He drew his sword and plunged out into the stench and screams of battle.

"For the land!" he bellowed. And everywhere he heard answering cries as fighters of Dread Mountain, Jalis, Mere, Plains, and Del fought their way to his side, and flaming arrows flew from the city walls. Strength flowed through and between the fighters for the Land of Dragons. Together, they charged forward, meeting their terrible foes head-on.

Greers and green monsters roared as the enemies they had thought were vanquished turned on them with new savagery.

Ak-Baba screeched with rage as the flaming arrows reached their marks. The arrows could not pierce the monstrous birds' scaly hides. But the flames licked at their wings, and their feathers began to smoke. As one, they charged the city, intent on destroying the puny archers who had dared to attack them.

Then a thunderous roar split the air, and a glittering dragon swept over the river. Its scales gleamed with every color of the rainbow. Its vast wings blocked the sun. The Gnomes on the walls and the fighters on the ground all yelled in terror. But the dragon had no interest in the city or the plain just now.

Belching fire, it challenged the Ak-Baba, the invaders of its skies. Instantly, the Ak-Baba wheeled and flung themselves at the dragon, attacking it on all sides, like a pack of ravenous wolves.

Adin heard the Jalis curse in awe. He knew that they were remembering words from the tale of Opal the Dreamer.

She saw the gray men that were not men swarming across the distant mountains from the shadows beyond. She saw a

"For the land!"

pack of foul, winged beasts attack a rainbow dragon above the broad river . . .

And surely, the next words of the tale were also echoing in their minds, as they were echoing in his.

She saw a city lying in ruins, and a great evil dwelling within its walls.

So we are nearly at the end, Adin thought. But he did not falter. For none of the fighters around him were faltering. Greel of the Jalis was on one side of him, battling a roaring beast. Zillah and Karol of the Mere were on his other side, fighting three Greers between them. Beyond them were Samuel of Del and Fie of the Plains, standing shoulder to shoulder with the young Del guard Walter.

They were fighting valiantly. And so were all the rest. But slowly, slowly, they were being driven back. The enemy was too strong.

Four of the green beasts were dead at the hands of Jalis. The plain was littered with the bodies of the first wave of Greers. But many other bodies lay there, too — the bodies of friends, of brothers and sisters, of gallant comrades. And the fresh Greers still pressed forward in huge numbers, guided in their every move by the evil presence in the cloud. They seemed to be linked with it, as the Ak-Baba were. The Shadow Lord, it seemed, had made improvements to his creations.

The forces of the Land of Dragons knew they could not win. But they would not give up. They would never give up.

Over the sounds of battle, Adin heard the high clanging of the bell. He glanced behind him. Perched high on the Hira wall, Padge was beating the bell as though his life depended upon it. Az-Zure was with him. She had torn off her helmet and was waving it wildly. When she saw that Adin could see her, she pointed to the west.

Adin looked to where she was pointing. He could see

nothing but struggling bodies, and above them, sun and sky. What was Az-Zure trying to tell him?

He glanced back at her. She had begun leaping up and down. And Padge was jumping, too. Both of them were pointing at him, then sweeping their arms to the west.

Their meaning was clear: *Move that way, Adin. That way!*

Adin shook his head. Whatever new disaster was approaching, he did not need to see it. He could not leave his comrades now.

But Padge and Az-Zure jumped even higher; they made even more sweeping gestures. He could hear the thin, high sounds of their screams. He could not make out a single word, but their urgency was plain.

Reluctantly, he edged behind Greel, stumbling over the tail of the green beast that now lay dead on the ground. He fought his way towards the western edge of the battle, not daring to think about what he was doing, or trying to guess what new horror awaited him.

And then, suddenly, he was standing on empty ground. He could not understand it. It was as if he had been sucked out of the fighting throng, while the throng had been abruptly thrust back.

Stunned, he looked over his shoulder. The battle was going on without him. Even the fighters at the very edge of the struggle did not seem to be aware of his presence, though they were so near that he could have stretched out his hand and touched them.

Or could he? For some reason, the struggling figures looked hazy, like figures seen through a mist, and the roar of battle was dimmed.

He turned his head again, to face the west. The sun was shining in his eyes. But he could see a mass of bright, fluttering colors sweeping towards him. It was as if dozens of giant butterflies were flying straight for him, skimming over the flat ground as the gray cloud of the Shadow Lord had done not long ago.

But this time, Adin felt no dread. Instead, into his mind came a feeling he well remembered — a yearning feeling of welcome. Was he losing his wits? He fumbled for the belt around his waist and gripped the topaz. His mind cleared and his vision sharpened as the great gem warmed beneath his fingers.

And he saw people of Tora, their arms linked, their hair streaming behind them, their robes fluttering like wings, as magic sped them to his side. Their faces filled with grief and horror, the Torans were staring at the tumult on the plain: the Ak-Baba savaging the weakening opal dragon and the evil gray-and-scarlet cloud brooding over all.

Wild hope flared in Adin's heart. As the Torans reached him, he saw that the leader, Lenore, was among them. Then he saw the two young men, Shim and Kayan. He saw Shim's father, stern in scarlet robes. And . . . Zara!

"Zara, you are alive!" Adin gasped, reaching out for her. "You — Shim — Kayan — you are alive! I feared — "

Zara took his hand and gripped it tightly. Her beautiful face was pale, and her eyes were like deep, dark pools. But still she smiled.

Adin tore his eyes away from hers, and looked at Lenore. "Thank the heavens you have come!" he cried. "Our people are dying. The Enemy is about to triumph. Make haste! Use your magic to —"

"We will do what we can," Lenore said through stiff lips. "But we have not prepared for what . . . what we see and feel here. Our magic is centered in Tora. The farther away from it we are, the weaker our power becomes. And I fear that the evil in this place is . . . almost too much for us to bear."

"Indeed," said Shim bitterly. "It seems we Torans are like flowers bred in a house of glass, Adin of Del. How beautiful and strong we seem in our own small kingdom! But take us outdoors to face the real world, and we quickly weaken and fade. Better, far better, to be a common weed, which at least the beasts can eat!"

"My son, you speak of things you do not understand," said his father in a low voice. But Shim turned away from him, and Zara bowed her head.

The death of Adin's sudden hope had struck him like a blow. He almost staggered. "Then why have you come?" he managed to say, keeping his voice even for Zara's sake.

"To give you this," said Lenore.

She held out her hand. On the smooth palm lay a huge amethyst, purple as the violets by the River Del.

Adin did not move. The precious thing he had wanted so much was at last being offered to him. But the offer had come too late. It was meaningless to him now.

"Take it, Adin!" Zara urged breathlessly. "When we woke at last, Shim, Kayan, and I convinced them that their decision to refuse it had been wrong."

She glanced at her brother. He nodded.

"How could we do otherwise, once we knew what a lie we had been living," he said gruffly. "The amethyst is the gem of truth."

"Take it, Adin, we beg you!" their father said. "Let our talisman join the rest, as it yearns to do. Let the seven gifts of the land be joined — at last."

Adin took the great gem and pressed it to the final, empty space in the belt. It slipped into place with a tiny click.

And at that moment, our world changed.

Adin felt a wave of heat flow through his body. There was a small, crackling sound. Then the belt blazed with blinding rainbow light. The gems flashed like stars, their dazzling rays streaming over the battleground, over the dark walls of the city, up to the boiling cloud that brooded over the plain.

Red light cracked through the cloud. There was an ear-splitting sound like a shriek of baffled rage. The gray mass seemed to shudder, to shrink. Then it began tumbling back, back towards the north, the mountains, and the safety of the Shadowlands, as if blown by a raging wind.

The Ak-Baba followed it, screeching like lost souls. The opal dragon, injured though it was, found the strength to chase them for a time, then decided it was wiser to retire and lick its wounds instead.

The new Greers, their master's strength withdrawn, began falling where they stood.

The people of six of the seven tribes cried out in wonder and wept for joy. But the Jalis roared in triumph, beat their armored chests, and began battling the last of the green beasts as a way of relieving their feelings.

And Adin stood motionless, shocked and filled with awe. No one dared approach him ... except Zara. She looked down at the wondrous belt — at each gem blazing in its place. Then she looked up at Adin's face.

"The gems spell a name," she said softly. "It is the land's name, I think."

Slowly, Adin nodded. Silently, he took her hand. And the light of the belt surrounded them both.

Message birds flew like black snow from the city of Hira that day, taking the joyous news throughout the land. And never had the feasting hall of Hira seen such a riotous event as the celebration that occurred that night. The cooks of the city made so many exquisite dishes that the table groaned with the weight of them, and even the Jalis were well satisfied.

If Adin thought of Opal the Dreamer's prophecy of

doom for the city and wondered, perhaps, if it would be fulfilled in times to come, he was too wise to say anything of it amid that general happiness. And the Jalis were too busy gorging themselves and drinking ale to think of old tales.

In time, Adin, the blacksmith of Del, became the first king of the united tribes of Deltora. And in time, Zara, the love of his life, became his queen. To his great happiness, they had five children, the eldest of whom was destined to wear the Belt of Deltora after him.

Adin was to rule the land he had saved long and wisely. He never forgot that he was a man of the people, and that the people's trust in him was the source of the magic belt's power. And this he taught his children, warning them that the Enemy in the Shadowlands, though defeated, was not destroyed.

Adin knew that by now the Enemy was cunning and sly, and had learned patience by his last defeat. He knew that to the Enemy's anger and envy a thousand years was like the blink of an eye.

So he wore the belt always — and never let it out of his sight.

Ballum of the Masked Ones

RETOLD FROM *THE DELTORA ANNALS*

And so I come to my last tale. Some readers will no doubt wish that I had not included it. They will wish that I had ended my history with the uniting of the seven tribes, the defeat of the Shadow Lord, and the triumph of Adin.

This is understandable. Most people like happy endings. And the tale that I have named "Ballum of the Masked Ones" is by no means a pleasant or comfortable one.

Yet I know I must tell it. It is a fitting ending to my great work, for it shows that one happy ending does not mean that safety is assured forever. It shows how the lessons of history must not be ignored. It shows how soon, and how cunningly, the Shadow Lord renewed his attempts to gain control of Deltora.

Direct attack had failed, and the magic Belt of Deltora now protected the land. But the Enemy refused to admit defeat. He found a new way to achieve his aim.

The way was slow and took many centuries to complete, but the Enemy had learned patience by his past mistakes and was content to wait.

I have pieced Ballum's tale together from many

reports and scraps of news in *The Deltora Annals.* Never before has it been told in its whole form.

It begins in the time of King Elstred, grandson of the great Adin, and goes this way . . .

King Elstred was a kind, comfortable man who enjoyed good food and wine and wanted nothing more than a peaceful life. His younger brother, Ballum, was a very different kind of man. Ballum was lively and quick. He could do magic tricks and juggle, and it was said that his singing could charm the birds from the trees.

The people loved Elstred for his kindness, but they loved Ballum even more, for Ballum had twinkling eyes and a handsome face. He mingled freely with the crowds in Del, delighting them with his tricks and songs.

Elstred was not jealous of his brother, however. He was proud of his talents and listened to his advice, for, despite his merry ways, Ballum had a great deal of common sense.

The only being in Deltora who wished Ballum ill was Agra, a gray, thin-lipped woman who had become Elstred's chief adviser on the death of his beloved wife, though no one knew just how she had gained her position of trust. Agra hated Ballum, since his advice to the king often disagreed with her own.

When Elstred grew plump with soft living, for example, and the magic Belt of Deltora was tight around his belly, Agra smiled and urged him to lay the belt aside for his comfort. But Ballum shook his head, reminding Elstred that the belt was Deltora's protection against the Shadow Lord. And Elstred heeded this advice, keeping the belt with him always.

It came to pass that Ballum had prepared a special magic trick for Elstred's birthday. The trick involved a casket that opened to release a thousand stars. But when the casket was opened at the birthday feast, a tongue of fire burst out instead of stars, and Ballum was hideously burned.

Who knows why this occurred? The few who saw Agra's eyes fixed eagerly, hungrily, on the casket just before Ballum opened it had their own ideas. But they kept their thoughts to themselves, for Agra was feared among them.

For weeks Ballum hovered between life and death. Elstred remained by his bedside night and day, nursing him devotedly, until at last Ballum began to strengthen and grow well.

But the beauty of his face was gone. His eyes, by a miracle, were still whole, but the scars of the burns were frightful.

Ballum could not bear the sight of his ruined beauty. He made himself a wondrous mask in the shape of an owl's head and used it to cover his face. People soon became accustomed to the strange sight of a bird-man among them, and seemingly life went on as it had before.

But Ballum's lightness of heart had given way to bitterness. He no longer played and sang. His popularity faded. Soon even Elstred and Elstred's daughter, little Princess Adina, became uncomfortable around him. For, as Agra often whispered in Elstred's ear, who knew what was going on in the mind of a man whose face could not be seen?

Then Agra found poison in a cup Ballum was passing to his brother, and called the guards, shouting, "Murderer! Assassin!" She screamed to Elstred that his brother wanted to kill him out of jealousy and bitterness.

And when Ballum saw that Elstred believed her, he gave a great howl of despair and fled, taking nothing with him but the clothes on his back and the mask that covered his ruined face.

He ran through the city, out into the fields, and into the Os-Mine Hills. He ate roots and berries, drank from streams, and slept in holes. Always he heard the palace guards pursuing him, and his heart was filled with hate for his brother, who had believed Agra's lies.

In time, Ballum reached the wilds of Deltora's north and found safe hiding. He was unknown in the small villages there and could earn a simple living by singing and juggling in the streets.

Soon other traveling entertainers drifted into his company. It was safer to travel in groups in those rough parts, and, having put his old life behind him, Ballum had slowly regained the good temper and lively ways that were natural to him.

He hid nothing from his new companions. He told them he was a hunted man, and that the king's guards might swoop upon him at any time. His companions responded by making masks for themselves and wearing them night and day. That way, attacking guards would not be able to tell at once who was Ballum and who was not, and he could escape in the confusion.

The trick worked more than once, and over the years the attacks became fewer and finally ceased. Agra had achieved her purpose by driving Ballum into exile and saw no point in continuing to pursue him. She now had King Elstred in the palm of her hand — and Princess Adina, too. And the Belt of Deltora was now kept in a glass case and worn only on special occasions.

But Ballum's companions continued to wear their masks in his honor by night and by day. They became known as the Masked Ones, and Ballum was their leader for many a long year. He married an acrobat called Liah, who could dance on the point of a spear, it is said. He worked secretly on creating masks that were even more wondrous than those he had made at first. And when at last he died, his daughter Sarah took his place and the troupe continued to grow and prosper.

Many centuries have passed since then, but to this day the descendants of Ballum and the first Masked Ones still travel the wilder places of the north.

They are a law unto themselves, it is said — a private, secret people with strict customs and ways unknown to outsiders. Many strange tales and rumors have grown around them. But few in Deltora now remember that their first leader was the brother of a king.

I cannot help wondering what would have happened if Ballum had never been driven from Elstred's side long, long ago.

Perhaps King Elstred would have kept the belt with him always, teaching his daughter to do the same when her time came.

Then, perhaps, Agra, and the chief advisers who followed her — all secret servants of the Shadow Lord — would never have gained their great power over the heirs of Adin.

And then, perhaps, the Enemy's plan to separate Adin's heir both from the belt and from the people would have failed.

Who can say? And certainly it is useless to look back, and blame, and wish that things had been different.

The past is the past and cannot be rewritten. It can, however, be remembered, so that its mistakes are not repeated. Truth will always be our greatest weapon against evil and tyranny.

In my own time, Jarred, childhood friend of King Endon, tried to warn Endon to wear the magic belt and mingle with the people. So Jarred was called assassin, as Ballum had been, and was forced to flee for his life.

If King Endon had known the tale of Ballum, he might

They became known as the Masked Ones . . .

have wondered very much at the similarity between his own case and King Elstred's. He might have refused to allow his trust in Jarred to be shaken. He might have become suspicious of his chief adviser. He might have put on the Belt of Deltora then and there, and gone out among the people, and discovered the lies that had been told to him from birth.

But he did not know the tale. And so began the chain of events that led to the second Shadowlands invasion.

It led to the Belt of Deltora's being stripped of the gems of power. It led to Adin the blacksmith's mighty work being undone. It led to the talismans of all the seven tribes being scattered once more around the kingdom.

And it led to another blacksmith's son setting out on a great quest to restore them.

But that, of course, dear readers, is another story . . .